The Open Sky

Michael Mawson

Acknowledgements

Many thanks to my initial readers: Helen Connor, Al Rhodes, Jo O'Brien, Nicola Fleming and Jeanette Palmer. All your comments and observations were very much appreciated. Special thanks to Helen for in-depth feedback and relentless encouragement. Special thanks to Al too – for assistance with cover design. Thanks to Vicky Brewster for editing – your recommendations for changes to structure, composition and at sentence level were absolutely invaluable. Find Vicky at vickybrewstereditor.com. Thanks to Sharon Mann for proofreading and for many helpful suggestions. Thanks to Lin White for formatting and for much sound advice in this area. Find Lin via coinlea.co.uk.

1

The Black Night

Si sat on the grass bank watching the goings-on in the park. Two boys were throwing sticks up into the branches of a tree over by the barbed wire fence, trying to dislodge a football. He watched as the wind lifted the lower leaves, their undersides breaking in pale yellow waves as they caught the last low light of the late summer sun. At the far side of the tennis courts, he could see Matty launching himself off a swing, marking the distance jumped by running a twig across the gravel. On the bowling green, Jay and his little brother were taking turns to kick a rugby ball up in the air, trying to improve their catching skills.

He was the first to arrive, so he laid back on the grass to watch the progress of the vapour trails across the early evening sky. The tips of three white lines crawled cautiously forward, advancing at different speeds and in opposing directions, inching slowly across a pale blue page. One line headed west chasing the fading daylight. A second, thinner line lengthened northwards, its barely visible metallic tip glistening like a late afternoon star. The third line slid steadily southwards, like the clearly defined trace of tightly handled chalk. He imagined this last plane hurtling over the Bay of Biscay towards Spain, the ocean below adorned with dancing diamonds and cut by a solitary container ship tracing its own vapour wake across its own sea-sky. As the trails slowly dissolved, like salts in sky blue bathwater, the approaching autumn term at school began to loom ominously on the horizon. The mournful sadness of the last week of the holidays suddenly took hold.

He'd spent ten minutes daydreaming and hadn't noticed his mates carefully aligning their coats at either end of the field. He adjusted his watch, twisting the leather strap around his wrist to check the time. Seven. Kick-off time. He walked over to the group.

"Alright, Si?" asked Jase. "We thought you'd fallen asleep."

Milling casually between one of the pairs of piled-up coats were Jay, Jase, Jules, Matty, Pete and Jay's little brother. Si's appearance had taken the group to an odd number, which was always a problem.

"Me and Matty will pick," said Jay. "If I have first

pick, he can have a roaming keeper."

The match lasted over an hour though, as usual, there were a few breaks in play. Pete spotted his dad passing by along the main road and ran over to talk to him. The game gradually ground to a halt as curiosity got the better of Matty and Jase, who strolled over to join the conversation.

Money changed hands and the game restarted with a dropped ball. Then Jase fell awkwardly, prompting the whole group to join him in a broken circle on the grass. Distracted, they began to compare the level of wear and tear on their pumps and trainers, pulling bits off and cleaning stripes and patches with licked fingers.

They sat there together for longer than the fading light would normally allow, restarting in the half-darkness that woke the lampposts from their daytime sleep. The bulbs rose slowly, their faint yellow glow at first too weak to pierce the gathering gloom hanging over the pitch, serving only to draw the darkness down out of the sky and up out of the ground. The ball was lost in the bushes. Jase kicked it out from round the back, and play resumed, but it was pointless.

They limped over to the wall that separated the park from the houses behind, settling at the well-lit spot near the road to the estate. The lampposts were now wide awake, sucking all the colour from skin, hair, polyester and denim.

"I'm going to the shop," said Jules. The rest of the group followed as if invited.

The route to the shop crossed the Wasteland, a derelict expanse of weeds, discarded household items and broken bricks on the opposite side of the estate road. The Wasteland rivalled the park in popularity as a hangout. There was always something to break, bend, burn or stash secretively for retrieval at a later date. On this occasion, someone had dumped several sacks full of building waste in the centre of the sitting circle at the far side. The sacks had already been ripped open and plundered, and the debris was strewn over a wide area.

Without agreeing aloud, the boys started to gather up wood and other flammable or otherwise interesting items and piled them up in the centre of the sitting circle next to the savaged sacks. They knew that the Wasteland was the one place they could light a fire where they wouldn't get shouted at or driven off. Even the police would just drive past and look over casually, knowing the small victory would keep the boys happy, warm and safe.

When the pile of firewood and other curiosities was enough to see them through the night, the boys trudged off towards the shop, checking their pockets as they went.

The shop was a short distance along the main road to town. It was now two-thirds dark, and the reflected light of a three-quarter moon shone like silver scales on the slate roofs of the terraces on either side.

Si looked up at the sky, as he often did. It was one of those nights when the stars above stayed home, leaving a scattering of solitary diamonds hanging lonely and low just above the horizon, shining ever brighter in isolation. Si fixed his gaze on a distant star. He'd been told (or had read) that when looking at a star, it could have died months or years or hundreds of years ago (he couldn't remember which). He knew, though, that this wasn't true. He knew that the star that he was looking at was millions of miles away and that he was looking millions of miles away into the sky, through the atmosphere and across space. He could see and sense all the space between. He knew that if the star exploded, right there, right now, he would see it flash and burn and fade and disappear – right there, right now. He wondered if anyone else in the world was gazing at his star, right there, right now. He wondered if anyone else was amazed by how lonely and beautiful it looked, hanging right there above the distant horizon of cold blue hills and yellow fireflies, right now.

All the boys went into the shop, except for Jules who stared through the window from outside.

The shop was long and narrow with a counter on the left just inside the entrance. On the counter, a low, layered tray held row after row of chocolate and chewy

9

bars. The boys overlooked these and focussed all their attention on the rows of jars on the shelves behind the shopkeeper. Each of the boys ordered a quarter, apart from Jay and his little brother who shared. A picture of a woman holding a bottle of beer leant lazily against the wall above the top shelf. It winked at each of them as they left.

Back outside, the boys all peered into and picked at each other's paper bags, chewing quietly as an evening chill stroked their necks.

The walk back to the Wasteland was interrupted by several stops: on walls, against the tree that grew from a circle of soil in the pavement, under the glare of a back-yard light, and lastly, in front of the newsagents. The newsagents closed in the evening but was still able to draw a window crowd, though its sun-bleached toys and fading comics were gradually losing appeal as the summer drew to a close.

"It's getting cold," said Jules as he pulled a handful of potatoes out of both of his jacket pockets. The boys all laughed, knowing what he meant, and knowing that he had nicked them from the trays outside the shop, and knowing why. He then wrestled a potato from each of the pockets of his jeans. To complete the trick, he hid his hand behind his back, only for it to reappear moments later, clutching a newspaper which he had fished out of the bin outside the shop and secured unseen under his belt.

"Has anyone got any matches?" asked Matty.

Upon returning to the Wasteland, the boys settled down on broken bricks and boxes, forming a rough circle in the dimly lit corner furthest from the adjoining roads. Pete and Jase began to separate the newspaper into single sheets, screwing each double-page into a loose, uneven ball. Matty and Si searched through the pre-sorted wood to find the little pieces and the thin, easily snapped lengths. Jay rearranged a disturbed square of stones into its original shape, creating a neat border for the fire. Jules and Jay's little brother sat unoccupied, gladly sharing their last few sweets and preparing for a more important role.

When the initial preparations were complete, Jules arranged the paper balls into neat rows within the makeshift hearth. He laid the sticks and shorter lengths on top, at angles and deliberately without pattern. A few of the bigger pieces were placed on top, slowly and delicately laid to rest so as not to squeeze the life out of the paper balls below.

Jay's little brother struck a light by positioning two matches at right angles to each other, pressing them together tightly just below the heads, and pulling them apart violently so that the clash of compounds sparked a flame. He lit a few of the little hanging leaves of yesterday's news from below. Everyone watched in silence as the flames began to take hold, not wanting to spoil the magic of the crackling and fizzing and flashing and buzzing. The hypnotic smell of the smoke cast its spell, petrifying all into fixed statues, emptying minds of all thought.

A stillness descended. The flames danced around the edges of the bigger offcuts, licking the sawn-off sides and whispering under the hot breath of the smouldering kindling. The lower layer of paper surrendered, imploding with the sound of crushed, dried autumn leaves. The rising tower of sparks drained the light from all around, plunging the world beyond its blurred borders into a forgotten, featureless darkness. Jules placed the potatoes into carefully chosen hot spots, pushing each one further into the heat with a stick he had set aside for the purpose.

Conscious there was nothing to do but wait, the boys shuffled uncomfortably on their makeshift seats, keenly aware of the vacuum created by enforced patience and the billowing hot air. Si felt like he ought to speak, to fill the emptiness.

"I'm gonna go to Marsdens in the week to get some new flights. Skull and crossbones, or maybe targets or Union Jacks. My dad has put the board up in the garage, and he says he's gonna get a new lightbulb so I can practise whenever I want."

"I'll come with you," said Jase. "I'll get something

with what's left of my birthday money. Maybe a couple of balls."

Everyone laughed as they were always losing balls. Sometimes they got stuck up in trees or were miskicked over the mill fence, which was too high and dangerous to scale, the far side too risky to get caught on. More often than not, though, they were run over by cars on the main road and dragged reluctantly beneath the front bumper, kicking and screaming against the tarmac, their dying cries fading as they approached the traffic lights.

The laughter died down, leaving a contented glow. The boys again gave their full attention to the fire. Si looked round at his mates, who were all transfixed. He liked them all. Jules and Jay and Jase were nice. He knew them really well. He didn't know Matty and Pete so well, as they went to a different school, but he'd got to know them over the summer holidays, and he hoped they'd stay mates. Jay's little brother was called Paul, though nobody ever called him that. He was a couple of years younger. Sometimes they called him Little Jay. Apart from Little Jay, they were all the same size, same weight, same shape, and they all looked the same. More or less. Just slightly different coloured hair.

The spell grew stronger. The whole of the rest of the world ceased to exist: all other sights and sounds, all other people, all other movements, the past and the future. Only the fire remained, viewed through a tunnel of emptiness. The boys sat quietly, happy and motionless, for longer than normal. Longer than the usual good judgement of a kid with a curfew. Jase's mum and dad passed by on the pavement next to the park fence, but he ignored them. They disappeared into the no-man's-land between the reach of the adjoining lampposts, reappearing briefly into the melancholy amber glow at the corner before vanishing. Si thought Jase looked sad. Everyone looked sad, though the deep red-orange-yellow-white lights of the dying embers had stoked a rare calmness in their chests. Si closed his eyes, smiling as he saw the outline of the fire projected from his memory onto his eyelids.

"They'll be ready," Jules announced.

Pete began to manoeuvre the potatoes out of their well-chosen cooking positions with his own well-chosen stick, rolling them into the darkness beyond the firelight to cool down. He double-folded seven pages of newspaper that he had kept aside for the purpose, rolled each potato onto the makeshift trays, and distributed them fairly and politely amongst the group.

"Cheers."

"Ta."

"Ta."

"Ta."

"Yes."

"Thanks."

The potatoes were hot to hold, even with four layers of paper for protection. The skins were dusty black charcoal, crisp and delicate like burnt eggshells. Matty and Jules took out their penknives, which they never used for cutting, to peel off the black crust. The other boys used their fingers, wincing as the hot, black fragments burnt under their fingernails. The flesh was hot and soft and stung their lips and tongues as they stooped to bite the exposed white insides. They didn't last long and didn't do much to ward off the hunger that always struck at this time of night, but the ritual was complete, and everyone sat silently in black-fingered satisfaction.

The fire began to die. The boys knew they didn't have enough time left to justify putting on more wood. They all agreed, without speaking, that it was better to save the rest for tomorrow. They watched as the fire began to lose its spark, leaving no visible signs of its former life as young, strong, vigorous wood. Only a sad, sagging mass of lifeless, burnt-out ashes, flecked with grey, remained. A flurry of screwed-up potato trays set off one last flourish as a burst of red-tinged petals bloomed and withered in a final swansong.

As the time to head home approached, the boys trudged to their customary meeting and departure point at the junction of the estate road and the avenue. Pete's dad passed cheerfully by on his way home from wherever he had been, wishing all a goodnight. Everyone responded with the well-spoken good manners they reserved for friends' parents and the odd teacher – apart from Pete, who stood in silent embarrassment.

Si looked down the length of the estate road to where the break in the houses revealed the western horizon. A faint red blush still hung over the brow of the distant hills, clinging stubbornly to the coattails of the sun as it crawled across the ocean. Remembering what he had learnt with Miss Walker, he imagined the estate road and the main road and the Wasteland and the park retreating eastwards at high speed, racing away from the light and heat of the static sun, hurtling like a rocket towards tomorrow morning.

"What we gonna do tomorrow?" asked Matty.

"Let's go down the moor," Jay suggested.

Nobody disagreed, so it was decided. Ten. Time to go home. The group dispersed in twos, except for Si, who faced a solitary trek to his house at the end of the estate road.

He hated walking home alone in the dark. He shouted his goodbyes to Jules and Pete, who were still in view, to delay the inevitable. The streets that fed the estate road at right angles from the park side were all narrow and confused. The yard lights served only to deepen the gloom of dark, hidden spaces behind walls and in corners and between houses. There were no signs of human life other than the faint, menacing sound of running water and the occasional ringing of metal on metal. The pointless shuffling of an innocent, inconsequential cat seemed to Si to be loaded with sinister, conspiratorial meaning. He began to run, his focus directed at the gold-leafed tarmac beneath him that raced in the opposite direction, back towards the park, at twice his top speed. He glanced to his right as the cold, dark stone gave way to more welcoming brick and wood, and slowed to a brisk walk.

Semis, warm and familiar, lined either side of the middle stretch of the estate road. Si knew the names and faces of the people who lived in most of the houses, so he felt at ease, even though he had never spoken to any of them. Bedroom lights glowed behind curtains, bikes leant against sidewalls, and top windows were open to the summer night. The garage doors, the front lawns, the corrugated man-made roof tiles. These were all the markings of Si's territory. He was nearly home, with just one last familiar fear to face.

Si's house was the second to last semi on the left, just before the estate road split in two towards The Birches up to the right and The Alders over on the left. Just after the house before his, though, running parallel to his garden fence, was the alley that led to the school playing fields. Si hated that alley. The well-lit gardens on either side, neat and ordered, seemed only to frame and emphasise the darkness beyond. The darkness of the school playing fields was a special kind of darkness – not deep, clear and empty like the void that hung over the midnight horizon, but unconvincing and furtive as if hiding secrets. Si had never seen anything beyond the end of the alley but had always forced himself to imagine that he could. He imagined movement: eyes, outstretched hands, teeth, blades, glimpses of foreheads and cheeks and chins, long coats, glass, the twisted branches of dead trees and the occasional flicker of flame. He couldn't run past the alley, as he was too close to home and the mocking disdain of his older brother, so he walked, his mind racing.

He closed the side door behind him, slowly and calmly and in absolute terror.

"Hi Mum!" he shouted as he flicked his trainers onto the kitchen floor. "I'm hungry."

Grabbing a packet of biscuits from one of the fitted cupboards, he proceeded to his usual spot on the rug in front of the electric fire and leant back against the sofa between his mum and his older brother, Shaun. The fire wasn't on, it being the last week in August, so he stretched out theatrically across the whole of the confined space between the sofa, his dad's chair and the TV, resting his feet on the tiled hearth.

"What you been up to?" asked his mum.

"Nothing."

Si loved this time of the day, especially on a holiday Sunday with no school to wake up for in the morning. There was always a film on TV, though he rarely caught the beginning, and he wasn't allowed to stay up for the end. He watched as unfamiliar characters in unknown locations took impenetrable plotlines to unexpected places. He didn't mind the not knowing and lack of understanding, and never asked for an explanation. He was content to enjoy the clothes and the cars and the accents and the bars and the buildings and the big skies. He especially liked the colours: colours that were only ever seen by other people, or in other countries, or in the future or the past. He let his whole body unwind and relax, not lazily, but with concentration and focus. He forced the day to slowly fade and float free from his eyes, chest, shoulders, stomach and ankles. He closed his mind and ears, the movie continuing abandoned. He shut the light out, leaving only slow, shallow breathing. He loved this time of day, though he hated that it didn't last longer.

Eleven. Time to go up. He said his goodnights as he closed the living room door. The street and garden lights cast a dim glow through the window above the front porch, tracing boldly defined shadows against the stairwell wall. Reaching into the void at the centre of the darkest depths, he switched on the landing light.

Tugging at the bannister with both hands, he pulled

himself wearily up the stairs, avoiding standing on the dots on the carpet. He filled the bathroom sink from both taps, washed his hands and face and feet, dried his feet and face and hands, brushed his teeth, and looked at himself in the mirror for a while. He stared coldly into his own eyes, combed his hair, tried a smile, then a serious face, then a frown. Yawning and on tiptoes, he reached for the ceiling, stretching the gnarled aches of the day into a smooth submission towards impending sleep.

He pulled at the light cord, glancing back at the mirror to catch himself silhouetted against the landing light, admiring his side profile. He put the landing light out, braving total darkness for a fraction of a second. Flicking his bedroom light on, he threw his clothes on the floor, pulled his pyjamas from under the pillow, and put them on. He turned his bedside lamp on, switched his bedroom light off again, and got into bed.

Reaching up into the lampshade, he flicked the switch across. Resting his head on his hands, elbows pointing to the ceiling, he searched the room for familiar shapes. His eyes strained to penetrate the slowly receding darkness. He could make out the wardrobe and the table and the map on the wall. A gentle yellow shading clung to the wallpaper above the curtains, gradually fading as it lost its grip on its path across the ceiling. The occasional passing car set off an overhead light show, angled beams penetrating the darker corners above the fitted cupboards, darting and disappearing playfully.

Si closed his eyes, though his mind still wandered through a maze of random thoughts. He needed a new school bag and would ask his dad if he would go fifty-fifty with him if he used the remainder of his money to pay his half for one of the nice ones he'd seen in Marsdens. He would get a shoulder bag this time. He'd keep it nice and wouldn't draw or write on it. His books would fit in sideways and wouldn't get all tatty and dishevelled at the corners, and one of those plastic ones would keep his stuff dry better than an army bag. A shoulder bag would stand up on its base too, and wouldn't just collapse in a scruffy heap in the porch.

He wanted to go on a big bike ride before the end of the holiday, as they hadn't been on one yet because of the weather and other stuff. He would clean his bike, as it was still muddy from riding on the grass in the park and through the puddles on the Wasteland. He'd put his new hand grips on too, as he'd had them for ages, but they were still in the packet. He'd tighten the brakes and check the pads and maybe take some from one of the discarded frames in next door's back yard. Brian wouldn't mind.

He couldn't wait to go to the seaside, and as next weekend would be the last weekend of the summer holidays, he'd soon be there.

He thought about school and about how it would be getting dark earlier soon. Then it would be autumn, when the dry leaves piled up in the bus stop, and they would splash around in them and kick them at each other while hanging around under the cover of the side entrance of the mill when it had closed for the night. Then it would be winter, and with any luck, there would be snow, and it would look nice, and he'd see if there were any plastic sacks on the Wasteland he could use as a sledge, and as the Earth orbited the sun, its tilted axis would mean they would soon spend their days in the weaker rays, that covered more ground, guaranteeing much colder weather as it got nearer to Christmas, and that …

2

The Green Belt Fields

Si woke and, as usual, looked at his alarm clock. Quarter past nine. He got out of bed, freed his dressing gown from the hook on the back of the bedroom door, put it on, and wobbled gingerly down the stairs. He took up his usual spot on the rug in front of the sofa. He was alone. As the sofa was unoccupied, it kept rolling backwards on its castors, which was annoying, so he decided to enjoy the rare luxury of sitting in his dad's chair. Unexpectedly, his older brother Shaun made an unwelcome, unanticipated appearance, slamming the kitchen door upon arrival.

"Why aren't you at work?" Si asked.

"It's a bank holiday," Shaun replied, as if it was the stupidest question ever.

Si walked over to the TV, switching it on at the socket.

Another film was on, which was unusual on a weekday morning. *"It's a bank holiday,"* he parroted sarcastically.

He tried to follow the film carefully. A man and his son lived together in an isolated log cabin in a forest clearing in a remote part of the county. They lived a reclusive life, keeping themselves to themselves and never talking to their nearest neighbours, who in any case lived miles away. The boy didn't go to the local school, and the dad worked felling trees, which were collected by a truck from a distant logging company. The dad hardly ever spoke, and the boy, against his natural instincts, and perhaps not knowing any better, was developing the same bad habit. One day, when the boy was looking in an old box, he stumbled across a faded photo of his mum, whose face stirred faint recollections in the distant, hazy depths of his memory. Overcome with previously buried emotion, he ran from the house and his dad and his life and the cabin and everything else. He ran as fast and as free and as far away as he could. He told himself that he wouldn't return until he found his mum, though deep down, he knew he would never see her again. As night fell, he was miles from home and hopelessly lost. He curled up for the night in the outhouse of an isolated farm. His dad spent a restless night frantic with worry. He'd seen the old box and noticed the faded photos strewn across the table, and suspected what had happened. In the morning he grabbed a sun-bleached photo of the boy and drove out to his nearest neighbours, hoping that one of them might have seen him, but when he showed them the photo, his neighbours thought that he had gone mad, as they were sure the photo was of himself as a boy.

Si walked over to the TV and pressed number three. Four children were racing each other around a makeshift obstacle course, searching for foam shapes, hurrying back to base, and dropping them in a sack held by a teammate. There was a red team, a blue team, a green team and a yellow team and each contestant wore a t-shirt of the corresponding colour. The crowd screamed, chanted and clapped in a high-frequency frenzy. Crawling round the back on all fours, he turned the TV off at the mains.

He walked into the kitchen and began to search through the cupboards. He didn't fancy alphabet spaghetti, or beans, or rice pudding, or vegetable soup, or Spam, or Smash, or stewed steak, or tinned pears, or evaporated milk. He progressed to the fridge, which was almost empty, but for two-thirds of a pint of red-top, a half-dozen eggs, a block of lard and some chocolate biscuits. He decided on eggs. He took a frying pan from the cupboard under the sink, cut a half-inch of lard from the block and dropped the lard into the frying pan. Turning on the gas feed to the left front hob, he lit the gas with a match, and reduced the heat to a barely visible flame. Positioning the frying pan carefully on the hob, he took two eggs from the box, placed a cup in the sink, broke both eggs into the cup (leaving the shells in the sink) and slowly poured the eggs from the cup into the frying pan. He took a plate from the drainer, pulled two slices of bread from their waxed paper wrapper, carefully buttered the bread with margarine, and switched the kettle on. He gave the frying pan a gentle horizontal shake to make sure the eggs weren't sticking and proceeded to make a cup of tea. He had a chocolate biscuit while he was waiting. When his eggs were ready, he served them up as a double, turned off the gas, and moved the pan to the left rear hob.

Sitting at the table under the living room window, he watched the early activity in the street as he ate. Matty was talking to some of the younger kids, as he often did. Si and Matty were two of that rare breed of older kids who were willing to give the younger kids any time. Two younger girls were skipping in the middle of the street. Matty took one end of the rope so that one of the girls could try for her record. As the girls swapped, Matty took a quick look over both shoulders to check that nobody was coming down from the park end. Si laughed in sympathy, knowing the awkward, embarrassed reluctance of doing something that you want to do but which others expect you not to. Matty stood as straight as a flagpole, his left arm down by his side, his right arm circling anticlockwise with restrained enthusiasm. Two younger boys launched a ball across the street, throw-in style, from opposing pavements, occasionally advancing to the white line to throw from halfway. Shaun vanished into the distance, having left unnoticed, fading from view like the dot that follows the national anthem, disappearing into his mystery world.

Si took his empty plate and cup back into the kitchen and put it in the sink. He decided to get dressed. His clothes were still on the bedroom floor, so he frantically put them all back on, throwing his pyjamas on the unmade bed. He quickly rinsed his hands and teeth with cold water and raced downstairs. He closed the side door carefully on his way out, knowing that he would only be allowed to play in that part of the street from where he could see the house, as his mum and dad were out somewhere, and he didn't have a key, so he would have to keep a close watch. He knew his mum and dad would have asked Shaun to look after him. He decided that, if questioned, it would probably be best to pretend that Shaun had very reluctantly agreed to go out only after having been eventually convinced by his little brother that he would be alright on his own. Besides, he was desperate to see his mum and dad, so he wanted to sit in the spot on the garden wall where he always sat when he waited impatiently for their return. Anyway, they would want to know where he was when they got back. His mates wouldn't be going down to the moor until after dinner, as only the afternoon offered enough time between being allowed out and being expected back in again. Besides, he hated being alone in the house, as he was terrified of the madmen and monsters that hid in the invisible space behind every open door.

Si sat on the garden wall in the gap between the sunken studs of two confiscated railings, picking dirt out of the tiny craters. He glanced towards the main road, hoping to see his mum and dad returning with loaded bags. His mate joined him.

"Chewy?" Matty asked, offering the whole pack.

Si grabbed the pack, took a stick, unwrapped it, folded it twice, popped it in, screwed the wrappers into a tiny ball, and threw the ball at the drain – missing. He gave the pack back.

"Ta."

Forgetting his sentry duty, he took up his usual position on the kerb. His mate joined him. Trying not to let Matty notice his anxiety, he began to fiddle with the contents of the gutter. He picked up a spent match, using it to flick fag ends at the drain – missed, missed, missed. Bored, he began to throw little stones at the opposite kerb, trying to land them in the gutter. Still bored, he gathered together a modest collection of pop can ring pulls, the type with twin slits at the joint between the ring and the tab, and began flicking the rings into the air with the tabs, using one of the slits to generate a perfectly judged level of potential energy. Stirring from his apathy, Matty joined in. Soon bored again, they instead marked lines on the kerbstones with bits of gutter gravel. This was much more satisfying, and both boys drifted into the timeless trance of carefree concentration with which humans have marked stone with stone since the dawn of time.

"Hi Simon," said Si's mum as she passed behind on the pavement half an hour later.

Si didn't reply, though he smiled in acknowledgement. His mum's appearance had been sudden and unexpected. His dad held a carrier bag in each hand, and his mum pulled her trolley behind. Resisting his newfound curiosity, he stayed put on the kerb and returned to his scribbling.

"You wanna walk down the moor, or should we go on the bikes?" Si asked.

"Walk," Matty replied. "The bikes will slow us down."

Si had no idea what he meant, but he didn't ask. He looked up at the sun, which was climbing slowly towards midday. It was starting to get hot, so he laid down on the pavement to feel the heat on his face and in his chest. Closing his eyes, he listened to the song of the street. A hammer, a radio playing in the neighbours' garage, the distant hum of the cars on the main road, voices from the kitchen, wind-blown litter dancing along the pavement, birds arguing in the trees opposite, the long grass in the lawn borders brushing against the garden wall, a motorbike on the quarry and the faint breath of the high, distant winds that carried the colourless, empty summer clouds from sea to sea.

All that doing nothing had made Si hungry, so he went in for dinner. Matty followed him in without asking. Si's dad was watching the cricket, which proceeded at bank holiday speed. At the request of Si's mum, Matty left to ask if he was allowed to have dinner at Simon's, and returned moments later to confirm that he was. The first course was little bowls of vegetable soup served with a loaf of bread. Si broke up three slices and stirred the pieces into his soup. Matty followed suit, dunking every scrap with the back of his spoon until all the bread was sodden and fully submerged. For afters, they had peach slices with cream. Si's mum pierced the can of cream at opposite sides of the rim so that the cream would flow freely. It wasn't real cream. Less than a minute later, Si had put all the dishes and spoons in the sink, Matty had put the bread away, and both boys were back on the kerb.

The street was quiet now, as the dinner hour was at least that (and often longer) for kids with no plans for the afternoon. Si, though, was beginning to feel excited and apprehensive about going down the moor, as he knew something would happen, and not knowing what only made it worse.

The kerb suddenly felt uncomfortable and unfulfilling, so he suggested to Matty that they walk down towards the park end, as he knew the others would be starting to assemble in the usual spot. When they reached throwing distance from the park, Si silently took the register: Jay, Jase, Jules, Pete and Little Jay all sat on the low border of rubble that marked the northern end of the Wasteland, ready and waiting.

The reception party set off walking before Si and Matty had a chance to join them, forcing the two latecomers into a reluctant stop-start sprint to catch up.

The first stage of the trek to the moor took in familiar sights: The George, the cobbled alley that ran past the mill cottages, the pony field (with its laughably insecure barbed wire fence), the quarry steps, The Wheatsheaf and the so-called castle wall. After fifteen minutes, though, the boys found themselves in worryingly unfamiliar territory.

A paint-stripped climbing frame in the ruins of a deserted playground provided a welcome diversion from the growing tension, offering the boys the first indulgence of the afternoon's adventure. Si, Pete and Jase sat it out, deciding instead to stretch out on the nearby weatherworn benches.

It was getting hotter. Si tried to decipher the direction of the clouds, though they were fewer and farther between than usual. At first, he thought they were westerlies, as they were a westerly kind of cloud. Suddenly, all movement above seemed to momentarily stop, replaced with the barely perceptible motion of the Earth below, which he thought he felt through his legs and shoulder blades. Then he decided they must be southerlies, as this explained their sparsity. Definitely southerlies, as this explained the heat too. Si loved looking at the clouds. He didn't look for faces or familiar shapes – what a waste of time! He loved big, billowing, bomb-blast clouds, with solid bottoms and gassy heads, decorated with diamonds and white gold and hiding deep, dark, impenetrable secrets. He was amazed by their colossal, towering power, by their contorted, shifting shape, and with the blinding light that they unleashed and the cool shade that they shed on the newly built semis, garden fences and closely-cut lawns below.

It was time to move on through a half-familiar estate where half-familiar kids that went to a half-familiar school continued to play without seeming to notice them. The roads were steep at first, becoming less so as they approached the bottom road that marked the northern border of the moor. The boys waited patiently for the bottom road to clear, then walked sensibly across, continually looking left and right as they strode from kerb to kerb. The moor wasn't visible at this point, as the upper slopes were forested with a thicket of trees.

The boys jumped into the depths of the cool, green sea that ran dark and deep beneath the playful waves of lighter-coloured leaves above. Si searched for a machete stick and, after finding a stripped and seemingly pre-used branch of perfect length and weight, proceeded to lash out at any hanging leaves and fragile twigs that got in his way as he thrashed his way explorer style through the thin trees and loose undergrowth that very occasionally blocked his path. All the other boys followed Si's lead, progressing in a slow, coordinated silence like a search party looking for evidence. Soon the trees grew taller, and the sun shone brighter, and clearings opened wider. Species became more familiar, with some instantly recognisable as good climbers, like sycamore and crab apple. Each boy began a three-part search for a climber. Part one involved finding a tree that would provide an easy foot up. Part two consisted of deciding which of the easy starters provided a possible route further up. The final decision was to select the potential climber that would provide the best seat and viewpoint. After several minutes searching and analysis, they began to climb.

Si had chosen a young sycamore, perhaps fifty years old. It was late August, so it was in its prime, thick with deep green leaves hanging tightly from rigid, silken branches. He tugged at the lowest branch, skilfully angling the binding on the sole of his baseball boot against a knot in the lower trunk, push-pulling himself up with his left arm and right leg to within reach of a thicker, higher branch. Clutching the target branch with the palm and fingers of his right hand, he powered himself up onto the branch below: left knee, right knee, left foot, right foot and stand up. He'd done the hard bit now.

He took a careful and considered look down, knowing that the dismount was the hardest and most dangerous manoeuvre. He took a casual and dismissive look up, spotting an easy route between close-set branches to a nice spot where a fork in the road provided a perfect lookout. He continued to climb, quickly and purposefully. He could enjoy this part now. Arriving at his chosen vantage point in less than a minute, he paused to consider his turning strategy. To swing about-face into a safe seated position was always potentially dangerous and involved trusting your balance and judgement for half a second of limited control. Completing the switch in a single movement, he nestled uncomfortably into his mid-air throne, his jeans pulling tight against his thighs and kneecaps. Searching the surrounding canopy for his friends, he was glad to see that most of them were still climbing. He couldn't see Jay or Jules. He spotted

Jase through a leafy window, wedged a little lower between trunk and branch at the opposite side of the clearing. Matty and Pete had chosen smaller trees but aimed to impress by settling farther from the trunk than the sycamores allowed. Little Jay was just below Jase, having traced his steps to an impressive height.

Soon they were all in position, and a temporary hush descended. Nobody spoke. Everyone knew that the lonely reward for climbing was best enjoyed in solitary, contented silence.

Si could see an isolated stretch of the moor beyond the top canopy of the trees, a little farther down the shallow valley. The moor was beyond their usual limits – a strange, mysterious, dangerous land without kerbstones, lampposts, tarmac or telegraph poles. A mosaic of fields, arranged like fragments of craft cupboard cardboard, coloured in every felt tip shade of gold, green and grey, stretched out of view towards the charcoal city beyond. Each carefully positioned tile sat snugly against its neighbours, its boundaries defined by hedges, dirt tracks, dry stone walls or the occasional row of desolate cottages and their outbuildings. A confused pattern of pylons zig-zagged in chaotic descent towards its final destination on the blurred horizon. The moor was another country, frightening and hypnotic. Si scoured the scene for danger, but the moor was horribly silent and still. Excited and afraid, he began to descend, drawn trancelike towards the open skies ahead.

Upon landing on both feet with perfect judgement and timing, Si was surprised to see that his friends had already assembled for departure. Pete led the way through the ever-thinning trees to the wild meadows that fringed the riverside farms. The group split up, each boy making the most of his newfound freedom to declare a wild independence, walking ten feet or so apart from his nearest fellow pioneer. They were over the border now, beyond the point of no return, forging a new frontier. The sky grew bigger, reaching out in every direction to unchartered territory. The air buzzed faintly, the grass whispered and the wind danced. Colours were different here, lighter and kinder and easier. The sun was still high, having just started its slow descent, though the edges of its cutting rays had dulled a little. An invisible calmness hung above their heads and beyond their reach, blurring the angled lines of the hedgerows and fences. They strode forward purposefully, as if in anger, until the black ribbon of the river blocked their progress.

The river wasn't really a river. It was barely a stream, but it was the only running water to divide the moor, so it was 'the river'. The boys left their sticks at the top of the bank and took up uncomfortable resting positions on the weeded slope that dropped steeply to the water. A million suns danced like sparkler sparkles on the cold, black surface, ducking and diving in uncoordinated unison like a flock of diamond seabirds. Bees hummed around the willow herb and amongst the dandelions, occasionally sending one of the boys into a thinly disguised panic by flying close by. The banking tops were decorated with sparsely strewn poppies, daisies and other tough, underprivileged flowers, creating an ill-defined border at the edge of their half-wild, semi-desolate garden.

The heat felt intense now, not because of rising temperatures, but due to overexposure, and Si was beginning to weaken. The boys rested, not out of habit, as usual, but consciously, with bowed heads and controlled breathing, with limp, outstretched legs and lazy hanging arms. Occasionally, the river would swallow a stone with a deep, hungry gulp. Si scratched around in the dirt with a lolly stick, unearthing a fragile, partially sun-bleached crisp bag which disintegrated upon exposure to the sun like a water-starved leaf. Golden Wonder. The sky was entirely clear now, but for a few organised rows of regimented high cirrus that hung upside down on the space beyond. A scattering of birds punctuated the clear blue sky above the far bank, nagging crows and a hovering kestrel: country birds. This was the best of summer. Butterfly time. The river whispered secrets as it slid past, releasing an instantly recognisable industrial estate scent among the reeds and banking grass which shushed in reply. The sights and sounds and smells of the ageing afternoon dulled the senses, leaving the boys lost amongst disjointed thoughts. Time passed.

"Let's go," suggested Jay, moving on without seeking agreement.

The rest of the boys followed obediently, tracing the left-hand bank of the river downstream with purpose, as if drawn by a primeval curiosity to chart the water's course. On the horizon, the bridge that carried the cross-moor road over the poisoned river took partially focussed form, floating above the blanket of heat haze that lay lazily on the mid-afternoon middle distance, gradually taking shape like a reflection in patiently calming waters. The bridge provided a medium-term target, and the pace quickened slightly.

Soon the boys were staring down into the water, a row of ill-defined heads lined up on a wall, bobbing playfully below a mirage of powder blue, the dazzling sky disguising the furtive black surface of the water. The bridge, however, was a busy place, attracting the walkers and riders and drivers of the moor's sparse population, and from a terror of moor strangers, the boys quickly moved on.

The attractions on the far bank of the river between the cross-moor bridge and Reservoir Street marked the extreme limits of familiarity for all of the boys.

Immediately opposite the safe side of the bridge was a plantation of trees which, because of its tidy rows and open spaces, rather than the availability of any forbidden fruit, was known to all as The Orchard. The boys automatically headed for The Orchard, spreading out in different directions at the limits of earshot. The Orchard was well known as a hang-out, hideout and unofficial dump and, as a result, was a great place for foraging.

Si found a partially shredded car tyre and a couple of rusted oil cans in the trees closest to the cross-moor road. Hauling them up to a suitably central but isolated opening, he began to create a seated focal point to which the boys could bring their weed-buried treasure. Matty and Jay dragged a huge summer-dried log into the clearing, creating at least three additional seats next to the tyre and oil cans. Jase collected drinks cans and bottles, lining them up with their labels facing the audience on a patch of dirt opposite the newly assembled suite. Pete pulled an old bike frame out of a tangle of undergrowth, Little Jay finding a few of the discarded parts nearby. Jules, however, returned with the richest haul of booty: a car bumper, two drawers, some magazines and a golf ball.

Satisfied with their efforts, the group assembled on the makeshift seats at the firing side of the range. Ten steps away, five bottles and seven cans were arranged in a neat row, like a dozen targets in an impossible fairground attraction. Each boy took his turn to throw a little stone at one of the labels, hoping to see it tumble back into the long grass. Matty took aim for the map of the world at the centre of his target label, though even a direct hit failed to knock the can over. Pete had more luck, his chosen label cartwheeling theatrically into the undergrowth behind in a flash of tartan. Si closed one eye to better focus on the double D on his selected bottle and drew his hand back slowly and dramatically.

Suddenly, a clutch of leaves high above shook with the sound of dry spitting and pencil-pierced paper. After quickly seeking confirmation in the terrified face of a friend, each of the boys sprung into a frantic race to reach the relative safety of the cross-moor road. Another pinhole puncture of the top canopy leaves echoed around the clearing, sending the boys into blind panic. Then another. Hanging branches were shoved aside, impossibly small gaps were powered through, and nettles were raced through with minimum care. Then another. Arms were pulled, backs were shoved, and shoulders were held in desperation. Then another. Skipping over the long grass, looking back, checking to either side, sheltering behind tree trunks, searching for a clear route ahead. Si heard the unmistakable sound of a barrel being snapped free from its stock. He realised he'd seen holes in some of the cans and should have known the danger. Brighter ahead, sky above, standing tall, slowing down. Breathe. Breathe. Breathe. A final look back. Short stepping down a steep bank, the boys finally reached the security of tyre tracks and footprints.

"Did you see them?"

"Yeah, I did. Think they were Westies. I'm sure I've seen them coming the other way after school."

"They're third or fourth years. Live down the Trinity, I think."

"Don't think they were aiming for us. One of us would have got it if they were."

"It was only a .22. Wouldn't have hurt."

"Unless you took one in the face!"

"I saw that some of those cans had pellet holes," Si admitted. "They were probably just shooting targets."

"Yeah, like us," Matty joked.

Everyone laughed, the last traces of fear and panic dissolving in the pits of their stomachs. Si sucked in the dry summer air, trying to steady his breathing. The pace slowed, though some of the boys made an occasional, brief backwards glance and half-hearted sprint. Within a minute, the group had returned to its normal pace, retracing their previous route on the opposite bank of the river, assembling to take stock at a spot over the water from their former resting place.

It was past mid-afternoon now, and the sun began to wilt and fade in its own heat, its paler, cleaner, kinder rays giving a Polaroid clarity to the tiring day. Si, though, was melting. His eyes began to stream like the unwanted stub of flavour-drained ice that clings to the lolly stick, and his head hung heavy and unsteady like a lopsided 99. His lips were cowboy dry, and his arms and forehead were starting to smart like bike-crash nettle stings. A chasm of hot air had opened up in his chest and stomach, its emptiness weighing heavy on his back. He felt like he couldn't go on, so he closed his eyes and lifted his face to the victorious sun in surrender. Fighting tiredness, he forced his eyelids apart, straining to see through the hot fog of the waning sun. Eventually, though, the shop at the corner where Reservoir Street met the road up the high school hill slowly took shape, mirage-like, as if focussed with the delicate clockwise turn of the dial on a portable. He checked his money pocket, his heart jumping as he felt the circle of metal in the cotton bag poking out through the exposed horizontal cotton threads of Shaun's old jeans.

"I need a drink," Si admitted.

The group crawled to the shop, dragging their heels in dishevelled unison. Si bought a big bottle of cream soda and unscrewed the top with his teeth, his palms and fingers too sweaty and weary to manage. Holding it with both hands, he lifted the bottle to a steady, horizontal position, sucking at the pale pink liquid with unnatural, greedy gulps until forced to come up for air.

He felt the cold spread through his chest and stomach and up into his brain, and he licked his teeth to savour every sweet drop. The shock made him cough, which he disguised with embarrassed laughter as he held the bottle out blindly for someone else to take a swig. Most of the other boys had bought cans and crisps to share, but Si couldn't resist buying a big bottle, though he knew it would prove an inconvenience later. Si continued to cough, the memory of the sugary bubbles lingering in his eyes, nose and throat. He was bent double and felt as though his body was repelling a sudden, unwelcome attack.

Jase had grabbed the bottle, taken his turn, and passed it on. It was two-thirds empty by the time Si had recovered his composure and returned to his normal posture. He rescued the bottle from Little Jay, who was, of course, the last to take a taste, and hurriedly screwed the cap back on. He was angry, though he was too tired and disinterested to show it. Taking a crisp or a sip from all of the others, he made some headway in recouping his losses. Having learnt his lesson, he took his time to savour all the other flavours: cola, lemon, tropical, orange, pineapple, dandelion and burdock. The storm beneath his ribs had passed, and the calm after left him feeling brighter and unusually content.

The boys returned to the fringes of the moor, taking shelter from the sun in the lowly ruins of the derelict houses opposite the industrial units, their jagged, shoulder-height outer walls providing just enough shade to cool the boys' heads and upper bodies. Si sat back against the wall of a one-time front room, his legs below the knee still basking in the heat. He clutched his bottle with both hands, securing it from unwelcome attention between his tightly clenched thighs. Hanging his head siesta style, like the Mexicans in the Saturday westerns, he swatted at imaginary flies. On the stump of one of the internal walls, he noticed a patch of well-preserved wallpaper. He felt like an intruder and imagined a silent family sat around a living room table during impoverished wartime, his TV drama imagination seeing in black and white. He pictured the wall in its original state, the room dark and gloomy and repressed, the wallpaper hiding dark secrets in its intricate floral flourishes. Feeling homesick, he took another swig.

The attention of some of the others had been drawn to an assortment of scattered odds and ends that had seemingly been discarded by some of the workers from the industrial units, dismissively thrown over the barbed wire onto the mound of earth immediately in front of the green chain link fence. Jase found a pile of freshly lathed wooden table legs, which he hid in the bushes behind the derelict houses, knowing he would come back for them in a couple of months. Jay had assembled a collection of roughly cut fabric samples, which he arranged into a neat pile, as they were brand new and too good to leave behind, though nobody could offer any ideas as to what he could do with them. Finding a clean carrier bag, he placed each piece in carefully, one on top of the other.

Si stood on top of the mound, peering through the fence into the yards of the units beyond. He'd never taken the time to analyse the layout and content of the yards before, though they looked entirely familiar: the pebble-dashed walls, the oil drums, the racing green paint layered thickly on the warehouse doors, the heavy hanging chains with drooping padlocks, the petrol-stained tarmac, the dirty windows, the random 'just in case' junk piled up between units and leant against the back walls. All were emblems of his hometown, out of bounds but strangely comforting. The dog in the nearest yard started to bark in warning, setting off all the others within earshot.

The boys began to tire of adventure, so they agreed to head for home.

"What time is it?" wondered Jules.

"Half four," several of the boys, all of whom except Jules had a watch, replied instantly.

The journey home took the boys up through suburban streets to the west of their original route. The houses here were bigger and grander, stone-built and boasting an occasional flourish such as the hint of a columned porch, a low mock balcony, a carved watchful owl or a panelled date stone. Cars soaked up the summer sun by the roadside outside every house, reaching unbearable late-afternoon peak internal temperatures, the textured plastic seats and the varnished veneer dashboards painfully hot to the touch. Cats lay like corpses in the shade under the bumpers.

The boys were silent. The heat was beginning to take its toll, leaving mouths dry, heads heavy, and arms and brows smarting. Si could feel the balls of his feet aching from the relentless pounding on the thin cotton layers stuck to the top of his insoles, the texture of the tarmac apparent through the inadequate rubber layers beneath. His eyes were getting lazy, and his concentration was starting to fade. He kept switching his bottle, now empty, from one hand to the other, sharing the weight of its inconvenience. His mind began to drift.

He imagined the goings-on at home. His dad would probably be sitting on a deckchair in the garden, listening to the televised test match commentary through an open living room window, flicking aimlessly through the pages of his paper, or perhaps concentrating intensely on the racing section. He'd have a tray on the lawn next to him, holding a big plate strewn with breadcrumbs, a side plate carrying a solitary remaining bourbon, and an almost cold cup of tea (two sugars and a drop of milk).

He'd be thinking about mowing the lawn, deciding to do it later when it cooled down a bit. His mum would be making her way around the borders, pruning the neglected plants and pulling out weeds. Or she'd be sat in the shade next to the kitchen door, listening to the radio and reading her book. She'd be watching for the neighbours walking past, as she needed to speak to several of them about a number of things. Occasionally, she'd admire the trees in the plantation a little further down the street, noticing the bunches of leaves in the lower branches swaying gracefully to and fro in the wind, like a ballet dancer's wrists, palms and fingers. She loved the summer colours: deep greens, pale blues and dazzling whites. Si was desperate to get home.

The last leg took the boys through a long, tree-shaded alley at the rear of the extended back gardens of the terrace of big houses that rose steeply, in triangle-tipped slate and stone steps, towards the neglected fence behind The Alders. Si didn't know anyone who lived in the big houses, though he had heard that the dentist and some of the teachers from the high school lived there. A silent gloom gathered beneath the canopies of thick-leafed branches that hung low and motionless in each of the back gardens, casting damp shadows on unkempt lawns and weed-ridden paths. The air was unusually cool and unwelcoming, though thick with summer wasps and crane flies. Each garden had a different rear border: sometimes a panelled fence, sometimes a hedge, sometimes wooden posts hung with netting. Unfamiliar ornaments like urns and statues and chimney pots adorned the mossy back patios, and all the rear windows had their curtains closed, as if hiding the sick or the mad or the lonely. Si quickened his step.

Very soon, all the boys were gathered in the gentle light and fading heat of the clearing at the bottom of the quarry steps. Slowly, they climbed like mountaineers up the boot-trodden, angled path to the gap in the fence behind The Alders, sometimes pulling on bunches of grass or clutches of weeds to ease the pain in their tired legs. Quickly crossing the finish line at the mouth of the path that led to Birch Crescent, they emerged triumphantly into the sunlit glory of the adoring estate, the majestic call of Greensleeves ringing out to celebrate their return.

An orderly queue had taken shape at the ice cream van, the younger kids impatiently walking on the spot as they waited their turn. They had become bored with pedalling aimlessly around the block, bored with overplayed kerb games, bored with their broken toys, bored with being imprisoned within the limits of the estate boundary fences all afternoon, bored with each other. Upon hearing the muffled approach of the electric bells, the younger kids had all run to beg their parents to relent, the excitement and novelty of the dissonant chimes breaking the monotony and misery of relentless sunshine. Most of the parents were happy to concede, as the kids had played nicely, and there had been no falling out, and it was so bloody hot, and it wouldn't spoil their tea, and it would do them good to cool down. The street fell silent as the younger kids focused on their Funny Feet, Lemonade Sparkles, Screwballs and, mostly, Single Cones. A few missed out, as always.

The boys didn't want ice creams or lollies. Ice creams and lollies were a sweet treat for kids who had been hanging around the houses all afternoon, popping in and out of their kitchens at regular intervals to get drinks and snacks. The boys needed food. Proper tea with a glass of yellow lemonade or iron brew.

"See you later, in the park," said Matty to everyone.

"See you," said everyone to Matty, though not to each other.

Si noticed that the garage door was open and knew that his dad would be stood next to the vice at the back bench, fixing something. He hurried over, carefully placing the sweaty bottle next to two others behind the front wheel of his bike.

"Dad, can I take the bottles to the shop after tea?" he asked.

"I suppose so," his dad replied grudgingly.

"Dad, have you got a new lightbulb for the lamp yet?"

"Not yet."

Hearing the reassuring cackle of crockery in the kitchen, Si rushed in to see his mum.

"What's for tea, Mum?"

"Your favourite."

Leaning over to the right, with his head horizontal, Si took a drink straight out of the tap. The water felt thick and full and soon began to sit heavily in the space just below his lower ribs. A stream ran down his cheek, and a tributary ran sideways across his chin, dripping in all directions into the sink and onto his t-shirt and onto the floor and onto the drainer. He dried his hands and face.

"Not the tea towel!" his mum ordered belatedly.

He climbed the stairs to his bedroom. His bed was still unmade from the morning, so he straightened the blankets lazily and lay on top. He closed his eyes and tried to shut out the day. The sounds of summer drifted in through the open window: a lawnmower, recognisable voices, wood on metal, Radio 1, teaspoons, running water, a bike chain engaging with the back wheel, flies. He couldn't concentrate on not concentrating, so he sat up, turned on his record player, flicked the switch next to the turntable, and watched as the arm lifted, shifted and fell, robotically. The comforting crackle of the needle closed the curtain on the world outside. Two rings of a cop show telephone heralded the start of the song.

Now he could relax. He lay back and closed his

eyes again, just him and the music. As the world faded away, he slowly became aware of a burning sensation on his upper arms, neck and forehead. It wasn't too bad, though. His thoughts turned to the evening as the afternoon was gone and forgotten. He'd spotted a bit of carpet on the Wasteland last night, and it hadn't rained, so if it was still there, it would be alright. There would probably be some cardboard around the back of the shop, and some broken milk crates behind the newsagents, and they wouldn't mind if we took them. And there were loads of candles in the garage, and Dad wouldn't be bothered if I just took the two-thirds burnt ones, and we'd probably need some brown sticky tape, but we don't have any in the house (I wonder if any of the others have some). We'll need some matches, and it would be good if Jase brought his cassette player, but I don't think he's got any batteries. I'll take a couple of tapes out anyway as I'll have my tracky top on tonight and I've got zips in the pockets, so they'll probably be OK…

"Simon!" his mum bellowed from the bottom of the stairs.

Si rushed downstairs for his tea. Corned beef from a tin, thickly sliced into three rectangles, with chip pan chips and beans. His mum and dad were having corned beef from a tin thickly sliced into three rectangles, too, but with tomatoes, beetroot, celery, lettuce, a boiled egg and pickled onions, as it was August Bank Holiday. A plate of corned beef, chips and beans was laid out for Shaun, too, and, as if by magic, he suddenly returned from his mystery world, taking his customary seat at the table with perfect timing.

"Where've you been?"

"The Feathers."

"What a waste to be inside all day on a lovely day like this."

"I wasn't inside, I was out the back. I'll sit inside tonight when it gets dark." Shaun punched Si on the arm, which would have hurt even without the sunburn, but Si laughed as it was well-meant.

"Si, have you seen the new W reg imports in the window at Millers? Black and grey with all the accessories?" Shaun asked.

"Yeah," Si replied, not knowing how to elaborate.

Si spread brown sauce on his corned beef and chips with the blade of his knife and poured himself a cup of yellow lemonade. Everyone ate without speaking.

"Can I have another glass, Dad?" Si asked, noticing that the bottle was three-quarters empty.

"I know what you're doing," his dad laughed. "Go on then."

Si drained the bottle and took it straight out to the garage, placing it carefully with the other three bottles behind the front wheel of his bike. He ran back into the house, hurriedly drank his pop, ran to his favourite kitchen cupboard, and took five biscuits from the open pack. He opened the fridge door and looked inside with disappointment, closed the fridge door, and took a carrier bag from the right-hand kitchen drawer. He inspected all the other overhead kitchen cupboards, took a milk bottle from the step, filled the milk bottle with water, and said his goodbyes to the family. He popped back into the garage to put the four empty bottles in the carrier bag, nipped back into the kitchen to pick up the milk bottle, and set off slowly to the shop, four empty bottles in a bag and a milk bottle full of water in one hand and five biscuits in the other.

The route to the shop took him around the fringes of the Wasteland. The bit of carpet was still there, so he dragged it into the bushes behind the newsagents in a half-hearted attempt to hide it from the younger kids. The carpet was beginning to fray badly on two sides, the thread hanging loose and easily pulled free. He realised that they could use the thread instead of sticky tape if they poked holes in the cardboard with a stick or a penknife. There were some broken milk crates behind the newsagents, too, as he'd suspected. No need to hide them! He looked at his watch. Five past six. Nearly an hour until the boys would reassemble.

He loved early evenings in late summer. The streets were quiet at this time of day during the holidays, as the weekday rush to cram in as much before the school night curfew was still a week away. He liked to spend some time alone, too. The sky was a blank canvas of bathwater blue, with just a few high brushstroke wave clouds left hanging behind from the afternoon, the lower daytime clouds having departed eastwards towards tomorrow. He stared at an empty patch of sky, forcing his eyes to lose focus so he could trace the path of the dust across the surface of his eyes as it danced gracefully around the void. He was amazed at how quickly the little dots and short strands darted to and fro, then realised that they didn't. Everything seemed silent and still. The weeds that grew wild and carefree in the neglected heart of the Wasteland stood rigid and motionless, like the plastic flowers in the library courtyard, and the bees and wasps and flies and fleas had all gone home for their teas. The leaves on the branches of the trees in the park hung heavy and weary and mournful and sad. The clouds were too high for the eye to detect movement. There were no cars on the roads. Si did a 360, but he couldn't see a soul in any direction. He felt wild and rebellious, his smarting forehead, dirty hands, dusty jeans and scuffed baseball boots all symbols of a day spent pushing the limits. He felt contented and fulfilled, so he took a bite out of the first of his five digestives, lunging it at it with his canines as if it were meat. He took a swig of water from his milk bottle, stopping to read the printed advert: 'Cool and Delicious Straight from the Fridge'.

He decided to take a seat on a stone in the sitting circle, as the carrier bag was starting to cut into his wrist. Flakes of ash on the remnants of last night's wood quivered like charcoal petals on scorched stalks. A disinterested dog walked up, sniffed his baseball boots, and walked off again. He polished off the rest of his digestives, guzzled the remainder of his bottle of water, down in one, and placed the bottle gently on the gravel. He looked straight ahead, focussing on the bowing necks of the long grass, the seed heads nodding and jerking like drunks fighting sleep. He lay down on his side so that the grass stood silhouetted against the trees in the park and positioned his feet so that they blocked the view of the mill wall and the first couple of houses on the estate road. Left elbow on the ground, he stroked his forehead with his right hand, the palm shielding his view from the houses on the main road. He closed his eyes and counted to three, opening them again to admire the artwork within his carefully crafted canvas. The pure and natural scene was short-lived, spoilt by a fag packet and the lid of a jar that he noticed in the foreground. Silent and still, he lay there for a while to imagine.

He imagined himself laying hidden within the shelter of a weeping willow, looking out through a window framed above and at either side by its slender hanging branches and arrowhead leaves. A clutch of long, unkempt grass that grew on the window sill hid his camouflaged face from prying eyes. Elbows in the dirt, he surveyed the scene in the clearing ahead, imagining movement in every likely position. He thought he saw a flash of colour among the reeds. His body tensed and tightened with a forced rigidity as if playing statues. Only his eyes moved. There it was again. A purple panel with yellow trim, definitely not natural colours in these parts. Surely some patch or flourish on an unfamiliar uniform. There it was a third time. Then, as the reeds grew thinner, the form took clearer shape as the back of a head and backpack became starkly visible against the backdrop of the white water ahead. A soon as it appeared, the vision vanished downstream in one of the many cleverly concealed river boats.

A helicopter buzzed overhead, briefly occupying both worlds as he reopened his senses to the surroundings. Back in the real world, he tried to decipher the make and type. It was definitely civilian, too small for a military aircraft. He watched as it faded from view, like a fly released through the kitchen window.

He decided he'd better get a move on, as he needed to get to the shop and back and eat all his sweets before meeting the others at seven. He picked up his milk bottle, placing it with the other empties in one of the collection crates behind the newsagents as he passed by. He stumbled to the shop with an exaggerated limp and affected sunstroke, though he had almost entirely recovered from the afternoon's exertions. He collected the deposits for the bottles, bought a mixed quarter of his favourites from the bottom shelf, grabbed a can of Pepsi from the fridge, handed back two of the four returned deposit coins, and secreted the remaining pair into the pocket-watch pocket of his jeans. He still had enough left for another treat later, which was an unfamiliar feeling during the holidays.

He opened the can before leaving the shop, taking his first gulp on the threshold.

"Lipsmackinthirstquenchinacetastin," he said out loud, as there was still not a soul to be seen on the streets. For a moment, he thought he felt an atmosphere of menace and abandonment haunting the shadowy doorways and open windows, and imagined a handful of tortured, cowering residents forced into sunless back-room corners, hiding inside in terror, fearful of every sound and movement from outside. He knew, though, that it was just the day and the date and the time and the season and the place that kept everyone indoors.

He strolled back to the Wasteland and retook his place on the stone throne. He looked around in all directions, repositioning his gaze with exaggerated and unnatural movements of his head and neck. Everything looked everyday and ordinary, and he was beginning to get bored, so he started assembling what they would need. He collected the broken milk crates from behind the newsagents, realising, as he dragged them reluctantly through the dust and gravel, that he had forgotten to collect the candles from the garage.

He popped back home to grab a few blackened stubs, forgetting the matches and the tapes and his tracky top and to look for batteries. His dad was rolling the lawnmower noisily over the concrete drive, unable to avoid the inevitable any longer.

Si headed back to his collection, pausing to pull the bit of carpet from the tangled web of weeds and tall summer grass where he'd unconvincingly hidden it twenty minutes earlier. Retaking his seat, he began to pull the thread free of the frayed edge on one side, winding the coarse fibres around a length of yesterday's unused firewood for later use. He remembered that he'd forgotten to look for crisp box cardboard behind the shop.

"What do we need?" asked Matty, appearing magically out of thin air.

"Cardboard," Si replied, knowing he didn't need to elaborate or give further instructions.

Matty sloped off lazily, also feigning exhaustion, pausing to lean theatrically against the frame of the paper shop window. Si turned from his frayed ends to belatedly offer his friend some cardboard collection advice, though Matty had disappeared magically into thin air.

Knowing they would no longer need the firewood that had escaped the flames the previous night, Si began to search the area for bigger or longer or thicker bits. Structural pieces. He put aside two long, thin bits and one short, thick bit. He returned to his unravelling and winding. Matty reappeared, balancing a neatly stacked pile of carefully flattened and precisely folded cardboard boxes on his head.

"Where we gonna go?" asked Matty.

"In the corner behind the bushes at the other side of the playground," Si replied. "We can use the walls for two sides, and it's quiet there, so no-one will see us."

Jay, Little Jay and Jase had noticed the developments from the park assembly point and were making their way over. Si organised his collection into four lots. He decided that Jay could carry the length of carpet, Jase could carry most of the milk crates, Little Jay could carry the unpicked carpet thread and a single milk crate, and he would carry the wood. Matty still held the cardboard boxes unsteadily aloft. His arms and the top of his head were beginning to ache, but he didn't want anyone else to share the load, as he'd been to get it himself, and he wanted to show everyone else that he could carry it, and it had been a nightmare to get up there in the first place.

Following instructions, the four new arrivals took Si's lead through the estate road entrance to the park, struggling reluctantly with their loads. Jules and Pete entered through the main road entrance at exactly the same moment, as it was almost seven. Pete approached the group, though Jules hurried diagonally across the unofficial football pitch, anticipating the final destination beyond the swings.

Eighty-five steps later (Pete had started the counting) the boys arrived at a clearing in the trees and bushes that marked the extreme north-western corner of the park. This was the furthest point from the lamppost at the busy corner where the main and estate roads collided and was, as a result, the quietest, least visited, most secluded, best hidden, worst illuminated area of the park. The air was cool and dry, and the first flickerings of darkness served only to exaggerate the punishing heat and sun damage of earlier in the day.

The clearing was sheltered by a low canopy of the unfamiliar branches and unrecognisable leaves of a smooth-trunked tree of unknown type (a non-climber) and was cut off from the rest of the park by a well-kept border of regularly trimmed bushes – the kind that are hard to squeeze between and that always leave a short pink scratch or two. The space between the trunk of the mystery tree and the right-angle where the two low park walls met was ideal. The landowners on the other side of each wall had taken measures to compensate for the inadequate level of protection offered by the stunted brickwork. On the other side of the low western wall, a broad-panelled, gapless wooden fence obscured an unseen corner of the mill yard. On the other side of the low northern wall, a tightly secured metal fence marked the rear border of the southernmost houses of the feared Trinity Estate. Luckily, the far side of the fence was shadowed by a neat line of thickly set conifers, so nobody from Trinity was likely to see that they were there, and even if they did, it would take them ten minutes to run round by the quickest route, by which time the boys would be quivering in terror in Pete's dad's shed.

"We might need some bricks," suggested Si.

Jules immediately forced his way between two bushes, as he knew there would be at least a hundred scattered across the Wasteland. There were a couple of places where they lay half-submerged and could be kicked or pulled free of the weeds and topsoil and wiped clean for reuse. Pete followed quickly behind, knowing that they would need more than Jules alone could carry, and aware that they had both escaped carrying duties ten minutes earlier.

Without coordination, leadership or detailed planning, the boys spent the next hour or so assembling the evening shelter. Jay cleared the corner of sticks and stones by dragging his right trainer back and forth across the dusty ground, flattening the sun-cracked surface in the process. Si hammered his short, thick length of salvaged wood into the moister earth near the base of the mystery tree trunk using one of Jules's reclaimed bricks as a mallet. Jase forced an upturned milk crate onto the protruding stone at the point where the adjoining walls met and jammed another upturned crate onto the crenulations on each of the sidewalls at points equidistant from the corner, forming a rough square with Si's post.

Si realised that they needed some cross pieces to support the roof, so he headed back to the Wasteland to begin the search. Little Jay tied one end of each of Si's two long, thin bits to each of the two wall-mounted crates and fastened the two opposite ends together, using the recently unwound carpet thread. He then rubbed deep, angled grooves into the vertical edges near the top of Si's securely planted short, thick bit with a caveman rock he found under a bush. This allowed him to tighten the thread around the joint where the two long, thin bits rested on top of the short, thick upright. This was the main structural strong point, so Little Jay asked his big brother to help him tighten the knot. Si had already returned with treasure and began to fasten one end of his newly found cross pieces to the midpoint on each of his long, thin bits. The cross pieces lay one on top of the other, so Pete placed the biggest brick on the sticky up end of the sticky up bit, securing the bent end between the big brick and the wall below. Matty and Jules positioned the flattened cardboard boxes in a carefully constructed, strategically overlapping arrangement on top of the newly built skeleton roof supports, windproofing the joints by gently placing the remainder of the bricks above potentially troublesome gaps. Pete repositioned his sticky up bit brick so that it sat on top of the cardboard above rather than on the wooden end below. He added another brick to make sure. Jay laid the carpet. It was less than half-finished, but it was as good as it would get for the first night. They all realised it was missing polythene waterproofing, some kind of side panels and indoor furniture.

As the crates had added ten inches to the height of the cardboard ceiling, the boys could all sit comfortably upright inside, backs against the walls. Si retrieved his candle stubs from under the bush where he had hidden them earlier, requesting a light with a shrug and a familiar look as he returned to the group. Little Jay still had the crushed box of last night's matches in his pocket, so he lit the wicks one by one as Si held the stubs horizontally. Matty took charge of the candles once each flame had taken, like an altar boy, sticking the base of each to a dollop of hot wax he had let drip onto a suitably shaped stone. He distributed the stones fairly and at regular intervals in the shallow hollows bordering the outward-facing edges of the carpet. Jase disappeared through a gap in the bushes, knowing that the flames had better not be visible from the playground. He returned, shaking his head.

The candles had brought on the night, and all was black beyond the yellow bubble which they all shuffled to stay within. The flames ducked and dived erratically in the fitful breeze and danced in exotic, reflected abandon in each of the fixated boys' eyes. The light, though, failed to draw the magic out of the furtive darkness that stalked every night, coming and going at will. They were neither indoor nor outdoor candles, but trod an unsatisfying line between the two, unsuccessful in their aim of dispelling the continual fear of the Trinity estate at their backs. Pete blew them out.

The night was all fuzzy. The heat haze of earlier in the day had chilled but was still hanging around, blurring all the edges and dulling the eyesight. Not a breath of wind nudged the leaves on the bushes or pushed the border grass back against the mill wall. In the stillness of the half-light left over from the candles, objects began to slowly take form, coalescing gradually into recognisable shapes, like the paintings painted on teatime TV. The fuzz began to dissipate, resting invisibly on the ground, awaiting reawakening late the following morning. Black bits became blacker, grey bits greyer, light bits lighter, lines better defined, edges sharper, shadows deeper.

The boys all sat facing forward, heads raised a little, as if watching a film at the pictures. A four-fifths moon suddenly appeared. The seas bordering the shadowed side seemed deeper and darker and calmer than usual, and the splashes of white more brilliant. All the continents were clearly defined, and armies of moon clouds massed at the foothills of the moon mountains. The deserts of the moon baked in the heat of the sun, and the shining surfaces of the lunar ice caps melted slowly in the dazzling light, longing for the cold of daytime. Some of the boys had never seen the features of the moon so clearly defined, noticing (for the first time) a grey-black, grey-white mirror Earth.

Forcing their way through the thick-set bushes bordering the dog walkers' pathway, the boys left their evening shelter behind, dissatisfied with the lack of side panels and the privacy they would offer, and resolving to make the necessary adjustments the following night. Most of the group headed straight for the playground, though Jules and Jase paused to chat in one of the spots where adults made small talk when their paths cross during routine evening strolls.

Si liked hanging in the playground after dark. He headed straight for the swings, hoping his enthusiasm to arrive first would go unnoticed. The chains had long lost the slowly absorbed heat of late afternoon and were wet and cold to the touch. He leant back, pulled back, sat up, waited, leant back, pulled back, sat up, waited, leant back, pulled back, sat up, waited. Soon he was three-quarters to horizontal. Featureless shapes in colourless shades flashed in front and above and below and behind and to either side, like front pouch negatives scanned hurriedly and at close range.

As he couldn't get any higher, he stopped trying. He locked his fingers together, his arms forming a tight circle around the chains. He tried to maintain perfect stillness, so the only movement was that of the bowling green ahead swinging in and out of focus. In the stillness and silence, his mind began to wander. Through his fixed gaze, the world seemed like a dream, or at least like a dream as shown in a late-night TV mystery or teenage horror movie. Si lost all sense of reality, imagining a world of mystery, intrigue, curiosity and fantasy. He thought about walking on the moon and looking back at Earth in terror. He thought about thrashing through the jungle, cutting bamboo to size with a gun barrel scythe. He thought about riding a horse along cliff tops, scanning the water for enemy ships as the moon pulled the starlit sea out towards France.

"Spin me," suggested Jay, waking Si from his nighttime daydream. As his swing had long hung motionless, Si duly obliged, shoving the bars of the roundabout clockwise with as much force as he could muster. Jay and Little Jay span madly in a whirlwind blur of blackboard black and white chalk white. Si, though, was starting to get hungry, and all recent thoughts of magic and romance were forgotten.

"Let's go sit by the lights," he suggested to no-one in particular. Everyone silently agreed with genuine unspoken enthusiasm.

On the return journey across the unofficial football pitch, Jay and Little Jay broke from the group, giving their apologies and goodbyes. They hadn't asked for confirmation of plans for tomorrow, which was unusual. It seemed everyone was happy to play it by ear when it came to meeting times and provisional plans, with it being so late in the holiday.

The remnants of the group exited the park through the main road entrance, turning left onto the pavement that led to the Junction crossroads. The stretch of road bordering the park wall seemed bright and busy, the car lights and pedestrian footsteps conjuring a sense of urgency at odds with the prevailing mood of the day. The route to the lights was lined midway and at either side with a clutch of roadside trees. The upper reaches were black and featureless and hung full, heavy and unseen, in sharp contrast to the supporting cast of partially stripped, semi-naked, yellow-tinged trunks below. Like dishevelled soldiers disturbed prematurely from their sleep, they saluted the passing cars with a forced, shabby uniformity, the overhanging branches creating a ceremonial arch directing all to the bright lights and muted excitement beyond.

The boys took up position on a low, sheltered wall that hung back at a safe distance from the unforgiving glare of the signals. Half-leaning, half-sitting on the cold, smooth, familiar stone, they rested in silence as the constantly changing colours induced in each a half-exhausted, partially hypnotised state. Perfectly aligned rows of cars, vans and buses stop-started stop-started stop-started constantly in patient obedience, further heightening the sense of detachment and impartial observance that had begun to permeate the group. Some of the boys began to blink constantly with the wide-eyed wonder of too-tired eyes. On red, the light softened the mood as the cars on the adjoining stretch of road ground to a halt and purred softly, like sleeping cats. Amber was the warning light, startling the boys from their submission to sleep like the big light in the front room when flicked on at breakfast time. On green, the boys all faked alertness, sit-leaning up a little straighter and lazily observing the moving traffic, longing for the return of soothing red.

"Let's get some chips," Si suggested in an attempt to break the spell.

None of the other boys had any money, so Si agreed

to buy two bags for them all to share.

Matty agreed to do the honours, as there was no point in everybody going. Si fished the remaining two bottle deposit coins from the watch pocket of his jeans and dropped them into Matty's cupped left hand.

"Keep the change!" Si shouted as his mate stepped onto the kerb opposite, knowing full well that there wouldn't be any.

Matty returned five minutes later with two opened bags, held with disproportionate care, like a cartoon villain carrying fragile stolen treasure. The boys took patient turns in taking single chips, no one wanting to appear greedy or give the impression of taking more than their fair share. The chips were just right, not fresh out and too hard and hot, nor a bottom of the tray batch, all cold and soggy. When each bag was half eaten, and the sharp edge of hunger had begun to dull a little, the boys began to pick more slowly, and the magic of the light show hung in the air once more.

The scene seemed magical to Si. The brilliant whites of the shop window lights, the red- yellow-blue-green-orange-pink flashes of the takeaway signs, the constant stream of the headlight beams, the dull golden monotone of the lamppost bulbs, the murky waters of the blue-tinged, grey-black, light-polluted sky. This was the mystery of the night. This was the closest they came to recreating the mood of the movies where important people drove down bustling streets doing interesting things. This was the high life. This was it.

Si reached for a chip, but they had all gone. He picked up the sodden newspaper and drank the last dregs of the vinegar from the grease-proof bag, wincing as the acid burned in his throat and heart, stifling the natural physical reaction like a bad actor playing a bad businessman drinking bad Scotch on bad daytime TV. Pubgoers had begun to return from their bank holiday bonus night, and the queues in the takeaways began to get longer. This was one of the many unwritten visual cues to head off home, like a police car driving by at an unnaturally slow speed or the living room lights going off in houses at the park end of the estate road or stray dogs walking in the middle of the street.

The five remaining boys dragged themselves up off the wall and hung a right, back towards the hushed familiarity of the estate. The park had finished for the day, turned off the lights and gone to bed. It was dropping cold now, and Si began to shiver in his shirtsleeves, regretting forgetting his tracky top.

Pete started to employ delaying tactics, hoping to put off the moment of mournful resignation which never failed to hit home upon the sound of the side door locking into its casing behind him. He stopped to address the group, knowing that they would all stop too, a strategy he only ever employed on the late-night return home.

"I know where we can get some pallets. We could bang sticks into the ground and then stand the pallets on the sticks. There's still some sticks over there. We could stuff the gaps with bits of bushes and leaves and stuff, and we could hang branches over the sides. If we got some polythene, we could hold it down with bricks and put branches and stuff on top and tie them together. It would look like proper camouflage," he suggested.

"Where?" asked Matty.

"They're behind the carpet place," Pete replied.

"They'll fall down," warned Si.

"Not if they were leant over a bit and we tied them together. If we tied the two sides together, they'd hold each other up. We'd only need six. There's some broken ones chucked out the back. They're only broken on the bottom, though, so we could face the top sides inwards. They won't mind if we take them. They'll get taken soon anyway when we start collecting. There's some other stuff there, too, that we could use for chairs and stuff. The gate's always open. People walk through to the hospital. They're not bothered!" Pete added.

"OK. Tomorrow," someone agreed.

The rest of the group continued their slow trudge home, leaving Pete behind. Si looked back. He could tell that Pete was searching for something else to say, to delay the group further, but that he couldn't think of anything. He laughed at Pete's theatrical stance, hands on hips and head tilted to one side. Pete laughed back, partly in embarrassment, partly in recognition of their shared understanding, and ran to catch up.

In the meantime, Jules and Jase had broken from the group and forged ahead into an unassailable lead. Si knew that, without a word of goodbye, or a thought for tomorrow, or a second thought for the endeavour, adventure and companionship that had gone before, they had resigned themselves to the inevitability of cereal and sleep. He shouted his farewells to his departing comrades, though they didn't look back. Si felt hurt. Hi liked good manners (hellos and goodbyes, pleases and thank yous, thoughtfulness and kindness) and was always a bit upset when they went unused or were neglected. He was quite tough, though, and shook it off like he did all the other little wrongs, injustices and defeats of every single day.

Matty, Pete and Si were the last men standing. Pete again tried to delay the inevitable.

"I've got no brakes. I only had one anyway, and the cable head snapped off," he moaned.

"Bring a bike spanner out," Si suggested. "There's some brakes on the frames chucked out in next door's back yard. All we'll have to do is loosen the nut on the back brake, and then you can unhook the head from the lever and pull the cable out. Or we could do both if you want a front brake too. I'm gonna get the pads for my bike. I'll ask Mum to ask Brian. They've been there ages."

"Ha!" Pete laughed in reply. "My pads are fine cos I've got no brakes!"

Si and Matty laughed in sympathy. The lightness of the moment provided the perfect opportunity for a parting of the ways by dispelling the occasional awkwardness and embarrassment that permeated such exchanges.

"See ya," said Matty.

"See ya," said Pete.

"See ya," said Si.

Si watched Pete and Matty disappear behind hedges into their respective adjoining gardens. He was alone again.

He turned to face the western horizon, still lit faintly by the recent death of the day, the sun having begun its silent journey across the ocean towards America, on its way to China, bound for Russia, chasing the morning. The road home formed a golden triangle, The Birches and The Alders barely visible at either flank of the distant tip. Si took a deep breath, his chest rising and retreating in resigned acceptance of the inevitable fears to be conquered on the journey home. He ran at top speed, and was soon taking comfort from the meagre delights of his second favourite kitchen cupboard.

"Hayo," he shouted, his speech distorted by

digestives.

Entering unnoticed into the living room, Si was confronted with an unfamiliar scene. Though sat in their usual places, the rest of the family were talking and laughing and smiling and coughing and interrupting and listening and agreeing – with the telly off! They seemed unusually animated, sitting on the edges of the sofa and chair, gesturing with their arms and nodding enthusiastically.

"Do you remember when we went to that caravan and Dad lost the key and we had to walk miles to get to a phone box? And then when the man answered, he said to go to the caravan next to ours for a spare key?" asked Shaun.

Everyone laughed, except Si, who couldn't remember.

"Then Dad had to pay a quid for the new key, and he found the old one in one of the pockets of his holiday bag."

"We never went anywhere without him taking that bloody bag," Mum complained. "It was only the patches that held it together, scruffy thing."

"Still got it! Last for years will that bag," Dad boasted. "Wouldn't give me my quid back, though."

Everyone laughed again, except Si, who was beginning to feel a bit out of place. He sloped slowly behind the sofa in the direction of the door to the stairs, wondering if anyone had even noticed him.

"Night, Simon!" everyone called in chorus.

Si quickly completed his bedtime routine and, within five minutes, was laid under the covers, adjusting to the darkness. His mind was empty. He tried to concentrate on something useful and practical but couldn't. He remembered what Pete had said about the pallets, trying to imagine how they could best use them, but moments later, they were gone. Then he thought about the trip to Marsdens, thinking he might go tomorrow, but it was too much effort to remember the details of his shopping list.

He lay staring into the emptiness, as all around familiar forms took gradual shape, emerging unaided from the clearing fog. Blocks and squares, randomly arranged around the walls, grew imperceptibly darker against the emerging, dominant magnolia, their contents visible only from memory, erased from view by the surrounding woodchip like the smudged stars beyond the streetlights. Just a few scattered constellations of letters shone clearly through the gloom. Si took comfort in the familiarity of the shapes, names which everybody knew and loved and shared and revered. Belonging words. Family names. Honda, Yamaha, Suzuki, Kawasaki.

3

Thick as Thieves

Si woke to an unfamiliar sight: rain. The colours of the
sky and the bricks and the slate and the leaves and the
clouds and the dark fir of the telegraph poles had all run
together down the glass canvas of his bedroom window,
like overwatered art class paint, and had begun to settle
in psychedelic, multi-coloured pools on the external
sill. Sitting upright, with the pillows arranged neatly
behind him, like a hospital patient receiving visitors, he
listened to the music of the morning. He closed his eyes
to hear better. Somewhere outside, he thought he could
hear the sound of the radio searching for the roadshow
(Si would always wait for his mum to leave the kitchen
before turning the dial slowly clockwise, silencing the
local news and edging delicately towards Radio 1).
That's what it sounded like.

Surrendering to hunger, he rocked lazily down the stairs and headed straight for the kitchen. There were two boxes of cereal in his second favourite kitchen cupboard. He closed the door, however, and proceeded to look in all the other cupboards. Disappointed, he was forced to resort to the bread bin, the biscuit tin, the drawers, the cooker and the coffee jar (which Shaun often hid food in, usually crackers). Further disappointed, he opened the fridge door and stood gazing emptily into the emptiness, transfixed by the blank shelves, white lights and exaggerated buzzing. As if under a spell, he lost a few moments in time, like when the bus goes straight past your stop, even when you're looking out of the upstairs window. Almost five minutes later, he returned to his second favourite kitchen cupboard, took a bowl from the top shelf, and poured himself a generous helping of Sugar Puffs. He grabbed the milk and a spoon from the worktop, where they had been left out, and poured a little milk into the bowl, stirring the mixture into a semi-liquid, semi-solid state. He put the bottle back in the fridge and, as he knew everyone was out at work, took up position in the luxury of his dad's chair.

He was still tired and a bit bored. It wasn't a frustrated, anxious boredom, though – he was too indifferent for that. It was a sleepy, accepting boredom. The kind that you can enjoy for ten or fifteen minutes. The kind that's hardest to break because you can't be bothered to shake it off. He concentrated on the wallpaper. He noticed a pattern amongst the roses, marigolds and exaggerated daisies. He'd always thought of the stairs wall as like an untended garden – wild, random and chaotic – but now he could see vertical, horizontal and diagonal patterns amongst the lemon, orange, red-orange and various shades of brown. He could feel yesterday in his ankles, knees, hips and shoulders, so he sunk back into his dad's chair, consciously relaxing each pair of joints into looser positions.

He looked at the mirror, hanging to the right of the stairs door, and noticed he could see cars approaching from the park end of the street. He could see people walking on both pavements, towards and away from the house, and see who they were. He imagined his dad sat studying the mirror, watching for his return at teatime, or on a Saturday afternoon or a Sunday dinnertime. He realised that his dad had hung the mirror there deliberately. It was a morning of discovery!

He walked back to the kitchen and dropped his bowl and spoon into the sink. There was a note, weighed down with a 50p piece, next to the drainer.

Simon nobody will be back until teatime but there's some soup and plenty of bread and I've left you 50p to get something else if you want to. If you're not going too far you can leave the door open but if

you're going somewhere tell Brian and lock the door
and leave the key in the usual place. Mum X

He decided to go to town and realised that if he got ready quickly, he would have time to call for Jase, and then Jase would have time to get ready and they could set off to town before dinnertime.

He raced up to the bathroom two steps at a time. He turned on the hot tap, brushed his teeth and rinsed the sink. He plugged and filled the sink and washed his hands and wiped his face with the cloth. He dunked his head in the soapy water and half-dried his dripping hair before washing his feet in the dirty water. He dried his feet and hung the towel on the side of the bath. He ran into his bedroom and straightened the blankets. He took off his pyjamas and stuffed them under his pillows and took off his underpants and socks and ran back into the bathroom and threw his underpants and socks into the washing basket. He ran back into his bedroom and took some clean socks and underpants from the drawer and put them on and picked his jeans and t-shirt and trainers up off the floor and put them on too before racing back downstairs.

Running into the kitchen to collect his 50p piece, a sudden thought brought his progress to a theatrical standstill.

"I'll need more money," he stated out loud. He stared out of the rear kitchen window at the pencil-grey expanse of ill-defined clouds high above the school playing fields. His money was in his top drawer, in the plastic box that his Christmas watch came in. He decided to take half of it, as he remembered his plan to ask his dad to go 50/50 on a new school bag. He knew that his dad was more likely to agree to put his hand in his pocket if he only had go 50/50 rather than buy the bag outright. His dad was a stickler for sharing costs where possible, and had once refused to buy Si a tent for £7.50 unless Si put in the £1.50 that his dad knew that Si had hidden in the button pocket of his denim jacket. Si put towards reluctantly, but then later that same morning his dad bought him a torch and compass for £2.50 from the Army Surplus Store.

Si rushed upstairs and took two dog-eared pound notes from the secret stash hidden in his Christmas watch box. He counted what he had left, replaced the elastic band, snapped the clasp shut, replaced the cardboard sleeve, and carefully manoeuvred the box to the back of his top drawer, where Shaun wouldn't think to look, and where the tennis balls, golf balls, bouncy balls, badges, belt buckles, old penny pieces, packs of playing cards, football cards, football programmes, football boot studs and broken watches would keep it hidden.

He ran downstairs and grabbed his tracky top from one of the pegs on the porch wall (where his mum had hung it). He quickly inspected the street through the living room window on his way past and hurried into the kitchen. He searched in disappointment in the fridge and the kitchen cupboards for portable snacks. He pulled the key from the kitchen side of the lock, stepped outside and slammed shut and locked the door, then hid the key under the plant pot next to the drain, and clambered onto the dividing wall so he could see and be heard over the dividing fence.

"Brian! Brian!" he called.

"Hey-ho, Captain!" came a reply from deep inside.

"I'm going down town with Jason. Mum told me to tell you if I was going anywhere."

"OK, Captain. Roger that!"

"Brian! Can I take some stuff off these old bikes? Just brake pads and cables and stuff?"

"Affirmative, Captain! There for the rag 'n' bone man anyway. Take what you want as soon as you can, cos as soon as I see him coming down the street, they're on their way."

"OK, Brian. Thanks!"

"Simon!"

"What?"

"When you've taken what you want, if you see him going past and I'm not in, will you take what's left out for him?"

"You're always in! But yeah."

"Insubordination from a Junior Officer! Intolerable!"

"See you, General!" Si laughed.

"Farewell, Captain. Good Luck with the mission!" a friendly voice declared.

Si ran to Jase's house on Birch Crescent in thirty-six seconds, knocking on the door in the hope of being allowed in out of the rain, which had eased a little anyway. Within the minute, he was standing on the doormat surveying the kitchen with exaggerated curiosity, as he'd never been in Jase's house before. He refused the offer to sit down, as he knew that Jase's mum was just being polite and she didn't really want him walking around the kitchen in his wet trainers. He wouldn't be there long enough to justify taking them off anyway. Jase liked Si's idea and went back upstairs to get the last of his birthday money.

Within ten minutes of leaving home, Si was stood at the bus stop with his mate. They decided to walk to the next bus stop, which was in a different fare stage and 2p cheaper to town. It had stopped raining, and a burning bright, phosphorus white, late summer sun was trying to negotiate its way through and past and around and between the clouds. The brooding cumulonimbus was beginning to ease and give way to cheerier cumulus, the dazzling light flooding the upper side of the transition zone clearly visible from ground level through the thinning, fragile, slowly breaking blanket beneath. Soon they were bathed in eye-watering light. The strip of weeds between the wall behind the bus stop and the cut grass of the rugby pitch was beginning to burn and give off smoke, and Si thought that they might have more rain later.

Jase was looking back the way they'd come, through the archway of trees near where they'd sat last night, hoping to see an indistinct dot of red coalescing on the blurred horizon beyond the lights. Si joined him, in sympathy, as he knew it was a frustrating experience. Although, as soon as he'd overcome the dizzying glare of the new sun, the bus unexpectedly appeared within the shaded frame of branches, trunks and tarmac, its number and destination slowly approaching focal range: 22 Bus Station.

Jase jumped on the bus and, to Si's disappointment, ran straight upstairs. Si preferred to sit downstairs if there was room but, of course, couldn't admit to it. He clambered up the stairs and took the seat on the opposite side of the aisle to Jase, on the second row from the front (the front window seats had already been taken, as they always were once the bus had reached the lights).

The conductor appeared from the back of the top deck. Si gave the conductor six 2p pieces, as he and Jase had agreed to and counted out and put together before the sun came out, in the knowledge that requiring change often brought on an intolerant response. The conductor knew without asking that Si was paying for both of them, adjusted the dial on his ticket machine, spun the handle once and gave Si a ticket, then spun the handle a second time and gave Jase a ticket. All without saying a word.

Si looked back to see if he knew anyone sitting behind, but the passengers in the rear seats were barely visible through the fog of smoke and sunlight. He sat upright, remained perfectly still, and stared straight forward, as he knew the conditions weren't right for him. He hated being in the confined heat and the blinding light and the suffocating smoke and the unpredictable rocking and rolling of the top deck on a day like today. He often felt travel sick, though he couldn't let Jase notice. He filed his fingernails nervously on the stubber to try to keep his mind off it. The bus was getting fuller, so he moved across the aisle to sit with Jase. This was usually frowned upon, but Si knew that Jase would know that it was merely the risk of ending up sitting next to a stranger that initiated this normally unwelcome gesture of intimacy. The awkwardness of the situation put paid to any chance of conversation, though, so the two boys sat in silence until the bus pulled into the station.

Jase led the way off the bus, turning to thank the driver before jumping two-footed onto the concourse. It was Si, however, who took the lead to the precinct, exiting the station by the pedestrian entrance and striding confidently through the narrow, shaded streets that bordered the Market Square, certain of the shortest route. The cobbles bustled with shoppers as it was half-day closing, and the mums and shuffling old men were ticking off their lists before the one o'clock curfew. There was only an hour and a half left, but that was more than enough time, with only two shops that held any interest, both of them in the same arcade.

The marketplace basked in the pre-midday sun, the shop windows at the western end directing light onto the fruit cocktail of flowers in the concrete beds at the kerbstone side of the pavement. The arrangements in the baskets hanging from the low, decorative lampposts were more vivid: yellow-line yellow, post office red, wallpaper orange and cricket whites white. Shoppers purposefully criss-crossed the Market Square, all seemingly bound for different destinations, all constantly avoiding potential collision courses, all with heads slightly bowed and arms hanging heavy and loose, all lost in trivial thought. Only the bench-sitters made an effort to focus on the time and place, the stillness of their legs and torsos compensated for with dramatic movements of their heads and hands. They seemed to study the shoppers with a detached fascination, like kids observing the random but coordinated movements of campsite ants.

Si quickened his pace to overtake the path of a

raincoated man, slowed a little to avoid a headscarfed granny, and was soon entering the Riding Arcade. Marsdens was halfway up on the right. Si entered and headed straight for the new season kits. He felt the material for quality and finish, studied the stiches for strength and uniformity, and analysed the crest for detail and accuracy. He was impressed, but the rush of enthusiastic longing soon gave way to a deflated resignation that he wouldn't get his hands on one of these for another four months at least, depending on the levels of Christmas and end-of-season discounting.

He quickly turned his attention to the more attainable. He inspected the display of assorted balls on the balls shelf: cricket balls, ping pong balls, golf balls, tennis balls, snooker balls and non-specific toy balls. Balls were usually an affordable option which at least prevented a boy from returning home empty-handed and unfulfilled, though they were not always the favoured or most useful option.

Noticing Jase admiring the display on the opposite wall, Si rushed over to join his mate. Jase seemed startled by Si's sudden appearance at his side and gave a nervous chuckle, peering anxiously over his shoulder at the shopkeeper, who was busy with his label gun. Arranged in neat rows and columns on fixed metal hangers were assorted boxes of darts sets, as well as separate packs of barrels, stems and flights. Si turned his attention to the flights. He'd decided last week that he wanted some new ones, and had mentioned it to his dad, who seemed keen on the idea. Si was having second thoughts now, though, but was reluctant to amend his shopping list, most of all looking forward to showing his purchases to his dad in the hope of approval. Being superstitious, he decided to stick stubbornly to his original plan and chose some Jolly Roger, Union Jack and three-ring target packs of three. They were 40p each, so he knew without a fraction of a second's hesitation that he would have £1.30 left.

He took his purchases over to the counter and gave the shopkeeper his two pound notes, which had been safely secured within the zip pocket of his tracky top. He decided that he'd rather have more change than pay with £1.50, as he'd once lost a pound note but had never in his life lost any coins. The shopkeeper gave Si his change and put the three packs of flights into a pointless paper bag. Si put the bag in the inside pocket of his tracky top, which he'd created by stitching around the bottom and zip-side edges of the previously loosely hanging pocket, to provide a place for carrying things secretly, like sticks, bottles and bits of metal that he brought into the house in the knowledge that his mum wouldn't approve. Jase didn't buy anything, so they quickly said their goodbyes to the shopkeeper and headed across the arcade to Goodalls.

Goodalls was mostly electricals, though they did have a small records section. Si headed straight for the carousel of paper-sleeved ex-juke box singles, as they were half the price of the picture-sleeved chart singles. He started at the top section of the facing column, flicked through every single in the section, span the carousel a quarter turn to the left, and proceeded to flick through every record in the next top section. After three quarter-turns and having perused the final top section, he directed his attention to the second row down and started the process again. After looking through all four sections on each of the four rows, he returned to look again at some of the options that had caught his eye, having placed them at the front of each section to ease this process. He decided to buy just the one single, and knew without looking that it would be 45p because he remembered with embarrassment stating to the group earlier in the summer that they were called 45s because they were 45p. He also wanted to keep more than 50p to spend on pop, sweets and snacks during the rest of the week, and with 85p left he would have a small fortune to spend at the estate shop.

He took the single over to the counter and handed over a 50p piece. The shopkeeper gave him 5p change and put his single in another pointless paper bag. Jase had selected two singles from the same carousel. Si suspected Jase had just bought the singles so that he didn't go home empty-handed, as Jase didn't often talk about music.

The dazzling light at the Market Square entrance of the arcade blurred the frame of the stone arch and whitewashed the windows of the first two shops on either side. Illuminated dust hung weightless in the air, like rocks floating in space, and random shafts of light beamed through the broken ceiling tiles, paving the flagstones with occasional patches of gold. The boys decided to walk home, not expecting the return of the rain.

Most of the houses on the first leg of the route home were big, detached, built from machine-cut stone (now blackened by smoke) and set back within spacious, trimmed gardens. Somehow, most had kept their railings. Si knew enough to know that most were over a hundred years old and had been built for the wealthy men of the town in the time of horses instead of cars. Si knew several routes home from town and could name every street and every pub and every club and every church and every shop and every alley and every landmark along each route. He took pride in giving Jase directions, which he didn't need, at each and every turn.

Once they had walked beyond what most people would consider a reasonable walking distance, they were back on more familiar territory. They were beginning to tire and get hungry, so they quickened their step, as it was after one o'clock and past their normal dinnertimes. Soon they were both walking along the single pavement of the estate road, approaching the point at which the route to The Alders diverted from the route to The Birches.

"See ya later," said Si as they reached the parting of the ways, prompting Jase to seek confirmation of the plans for the rest of the day.

"Dunno," Si replied, as he was tired and didn't want to commit. They parted with a mutual half-hearted raise of the arm in salute.

Si took the key from under the plant pot near the drain, unlocked the door, threw the key onto the kitchen table, and headed straight for his favourite kitchen cupboard. He took out a tin of vegetable soup and opened it with the camping box tin opener. He poured the soup into his usual pan, which was already resting on the front left ring (using a spoon to scrape out the carrot, pea and potato pieces that had settled and solidified at the bottom of the tin). He lit the gas with a match and turned the burner down to a very low flame (he had always cooked with a very low flame since the Valentine's Day chip pan incident). He took three slices of bread from the waxed paper wrapper, buttered the bread with margarine, poured the lukewarm soup into his usual bowl, and sat at the kitchen table to eat, like on a school day teatime. He re-read the note from his mum, giving a wry smile at the thought that he would use any of the money she had given him on meal food.

Having considered his options, he decided to stay at home for the afternoon. He knew that making arrangements for the afternoon might not be easy, whereas he would only have to walk to the park or the Wasteland after tea, and everyone would be there. He took his single upstairs to his bedroom, played the A-side three times, played the B-side twice, put the single back in its paper sleeve, and placed it in pride of place at the front of his paper-sleeve section, as he did with all his new purchases (the few picture-sleeve singles he owned were kept in the record box with his albums for protection and safekeeping). Knowing that he would have plenty of time to play records when the school nights started again the following week, he headed outside.

He was busy all afternoon. First, he went into the garage to test out some of his new flights, which were still in the pointless paper bag in his homemade inside pocket. He decided to try out the skull and crossbones. He removed the old flights from the stems. They were beginning to feather and split, and he was bored with their stripes, but he nevertheless put them neatly away in the plastic moulding from which he'd just taken out his new flights. He put the old flights and the other two new packs into the only drawer that his dad said he was allowed to use. He put his new flights in, noticing that two of the darts had a holding pin missing at the top of the stem but knowing that they would still hold true.

He practised for half an hour, frustrated by the lack of a lightbulb. The mid-afternoon glare of the outside barely penetrated the familiar, oil-stained gloom of the unseasonably cold garage. He put his darts back into the drawer. He grabbed his cycling multi-tool and headed outside.

He jumped over Brian's fence and set to work on the abandoned bikes. He removed all eight brake blocks, leaving them in their metal casings, as he knew he could use them on any and every bike. Likewise, the brake cables. He loosened them from the clamps, removed the heads from the levers, and pulled them out slowly so they wouldn't catch or shred. He unscrewed the dust caps. He inspected the frames, tyres and handlebars, but they were either worse for wear or non-compatible, so he decided that he had enough.

Suddenly a low but piercing *boom boom booming* made him jolt with terror. He jumped an inch into the air, landing with legs slightly further apart, like a sailor steadying himself on the deck of a storm-tossed ship. Brian was standing at the kitchen window, shaking his fist in contrived anger. Si laughed.

"Keep those eyes peeled!" shouted Brian through the glass.

Si put his thumbs up and carefully and respectfully climbed back over the fence, as Brian was watching, just to be on the safe side. He returned to the garage and laid out his booty on the concrete floor next to his mud-stained bike, which was leant in its usual position against the house-side wall. He took a bucket from his dad's cleaning shelf and popped back into the house to get hot water and a second-hand cloth from the tray of cloths that his mum had said he was allowed to use. He placed the bucket in the middle of the drive and wheeled his bike out into the blinding light of mid-afternoon, flipping it over, so it balanced unconvincingly on the saddle and handlebars.

He set to work on the encrusted mud, wringing the cloth out six inches above the upturned bottom bracket to free the cables from their sun-dried coating. He used the same strategy with the chainstays and the down tube, running the cloth under the cables to rub off the last of the grime. Then he rinsed and wrung out the cloth three times, giving it an extra squeeze before wiping the excess dirty water off the frame and cleaning the rest of his bike with the slightly damp, partially shredded remnants of his mum's old washing up cloth.

He carried the bucket out to the street, raising his free shoulder and leaning slightly to the bucket side to exaggerate the weight of the load to anyone who might be watching, then poured the dirty water down the drain, lifting the bucket manfully as it became gradually lighter. Leaving the cloth in the bottom, he returned the bucket to his dad's cleaning shelf, flipped his bike onto its wheels, and pushed it back to its usual position.

He set to work on the brakes. His pads were all worn down to within a quarter of an inch of their metal casings, so he replaced them with four of the blocks from Brian's bikes, which were as good as new. He tested the brakes, but they were a bit keen due to the extra width of the pads, and the wheels caught and whistled in places (they were a bit buckled, after all). He loosened the cables, using the pliers his dad had left on the workbench to grip the shredding ends as he tightened the nuts. His brakes worked perfectly – neither too eager nor too feeble. Remembering what Pete had said the previous night, he put the remaining blocks and cables from Brian's bikes into the only drawer that his dad said he was allowed to use for safekeeping. He took his new grips out from the tin hidden at the back of the drawer and shoved them slowly onto the cold stainless steel of his bar ends, holding them tightly for a few seconds and revving the engine with the right-hand grip. He stood back and admired his handy work, rubbing his hands with the cloth like a backstreet mechanic negotiating prices.

He closed the garage door, expertly pulling it down from its horizontal, overhead resting place, tugging at the bottom rim and avoiding the rarely used rope (the garage door had to be closed at a precise speed and with modest, measured power, or it would likely come off its rollers!).

He went back inside and made a pot of tea, searching through the pile of crockery on the drainer for his favourite mug, the one with the recipe for Scotch broth on the side. He poured himself a cuppa whilst it was still hot and before it got too strong. He took up position on the front step to observe proceedings on the estate. Two kids were playing with trucks and cars on the pavement. Two other kids were sat on stationary bikes, talking. Jules was sitting on a garden wall farther down the street, towards the park. Si could tell from his body language that he was otherwise engaged and wouldn't want disturbing.

Si felt strange. The scene on the street seemed somehow unreal, as if viewed secretly or through an invisible screen. The sun had gone in, leaving neither light nor shade, but a curious absence of both, like in a black and white photo, but in colour. The kids ran up and down and across Birch Crescent, and a car passed by on the park road, but the street still appeared strangely frozen in time, like a scene from a home movie. Si was hit by the sudden onset of déjà vu, feeling it most keenly behind his eyes and in his neck and across his shoulders. Just as quickly, it was gone. He almost doubted it had even happened, or perhaps he had mistaken it for something else. He couldn't shake off the feeling of being detached, as if he was viewing everything from outside, but from inside. It felt good. It felt like he was watching something that happens every day, but that the everyday happens every day, and that if you put all the every days together you get forever.

He saw his mum approaching along the park road, crossing the mouth of the alley that led to the school playing fields. He stood up and walked towards her, not wanting to wait the extra couple of seconds it would take for her to reach the side door. He took hold of her lower arm as she reached the gap where the gate used to be, not wanting to be seen holding hands. Hanging loosely but needily at her side, slightly behind, he followed her through the open door and into the kitchen.

Si wasted the next couple of hours aimlessly seeking satisfaction in completing various pointless tasks. He sorted his football cards into alphabetical order by surname, relegating the crests and team photos to the back of the pack. He numbered all his golf balls with a black marker, hoping there wouldn't be as much arguing next time if each player used a different number, and remembering that he could avoid losing the refundable 10p deposit again if he took his own balls. He wrote the names of his favourite bands at the top of the first few pages of his new bedside reporters' notebook, in preference order. He listed the band members below, and then the names of their albums, this time in chronological order of release. He was about to rearrange the order that his shirts were hanging in the wardrobe when his mum shouted him down for tea.

After a delicious tea of tinned mince, tinned potatoes and tinned processed peas, followed by tinned peaches with tinned cream, Si sat down to watch a bit of teatime telly. His dad and Shaun were back, so he was relegated to his usual spot on the rug. He watched without looking, thinking instead about the exposed soil patches surrounding the den and the tufts of long grass at the back of the carpet place and the permanent potholes covering the Wasteland, and wondering if everything had dried sufficiently.

He arched his neck backwards so as to survey the inverted sky beneath his brow, though he could detect no hint of a return of the sun. The sky had gone, leaving no trace of colour. All that remained was a monotone, featureless blank canvas, thoughtlessly occupying the space where the summer sky had previously been painted. He could hear the distant rumble of a plane approaching, so he jumped to his feet and ran to the window. The roar grew louder, as if descending vertically from space. He could see no sign nor detect a direction of travel. Slowly, the roar faded to a purr as the plane ascended vertically back into the upper atmosphere. At least it wasn't raining again, he noticed.

Si headed out for the night. He ran down the drive, through the gap where the gate used to be, and past the alley that led to the school playing fields, which even during broad daylight he was uneasy about hanging around. He saw Pete further up the road, so he ran to catch up. Si knew where Pete was going, so he didn't ask. He enjoyed how the boys often left things unsaid. It was as if they all knew the plan, knew what was expected of each of them, and knew what to expect of each other. It was as if everything had been agreed beforehand, and to seek confirmation would be a sign of weakness or stupidity. It was as if they were following orders, which had to be left unspoken in case anyone was listening. It was as if they had their own silent language, spoken only with subtle flicks of the hands and elbows, with coughs and whistles and with tiny movements of the eyes and barely visible nodding of the head.

All the others were waiting by what remained of the park fence, as Si knew they would be. Si and Pete were greeted with uncommon enthusiasm, so Si knew that something was afoot. Pete waltzed straight past the assembled group with arrogance and purpose, so Si knew that plans had been made in his absence during the afternoon.

Pete led the way down an overgrown gravel slope behind a row of houses that dropped gently from the safety of the park road to the barely known danger zone surrounding the rarely visited carpet place. Broken glass littered the weed-ridden, pock-marked, crumbling concrete courtyard that stretched out in front of the pointless carpet place gates, which were always wide open. Despite its apparent accessibility, the carpet place was forbidden territory: dark and mysterious. The strip of bare tarmac within the perimeter fence seemed unwelcoming and cold, and the corrugated metal frame of the almost featureless warehouse released an air of impending danger. Children had no place there and could do no good nor serve a practical purpose. It was a world where only the pointless and indecipherable actions of adults took place and where an unsuspecting child might disappear unexpectedly and without a trace. It was haunted by the living ghosts of the overall people, who were imprisoned permanently with the four steel walls, and only ever appeared occasionally at the solitary first-floor window or in the shadows of the roller shutters.

Pretending to feel no fear, Pete walked straight through the open gates. Heading for the bins around the back, he hugged the near side of the warehouse panelling, crouching as he passed under the window, as if this would make him less visible. He tried to make silent steps, not on tiptoe, but flat-footed, as if wading through water, the limbs on each side of his body moving forwards and backwards in unison.

"C'mon!" said Jase with a dismissive laugh, and the rest of the group followed casually, overtaking Pete before he reached the pallets. Six of the boys each grabbed a broken pallet, Little Jay instead focussing his attention on a small wooden crate discarded nearby.

Jules spotted something interesting hanging out of the metal bin near the rear shutters, and on closer inspection, was overjoyed to discover a mess of tangled polythene carpet sleeves. "Yes!" he exclaimed. "We can cut these up and put bricks on the overlapping bits."

The boys were interrupted by an unintelligible shout from the back garden of the nearby end terrace. A man was looking over the garden fence, only his head visible, and although appearing curious as to goings-on, he didn't seem threatening, so the boys resisted the urge to run.

"We're just taking the broken ones," Jase pleaded. "We're building a den at the top of the park. We'll look after them, and when it starts getting too cold, we'll put them in a pile on the Wasteland. They can be the start of our collection, and other people can put stuff on there too. We won't leave them lying around. Promise!"

"OK, boys!" the head replied. "Your dads will find out, though, if you leave them lying on the grass or something."

"We won't, mister!" Jase replied, safe in the

knowledge that whoever it was didn't know any of their dads and that they wouldn't dream of leaving such priceless valuables lying around anyway.

The boys retraced their steps back to the park road, each dragging a broken pallet, except Little Jay, who carried the small crate, now stuffed full of polythene carpet sleeves, holding it high up on his chest with both hands. Upon crossing the park road, Jay gave his pallet to Si and headed purposefully over the grass towards the Wasteland. Realising what he was doing, Jules gave his pallet to Pete and followed closely behind. Suspecting that it might need three of them, Matty gave his pallet to Jase, leaving the three biggest boys each dragging two pallets.

By the time the pallet bearers approached the row of bushes that shielded the den from prying, nosey, interfering, jealous eyes, the three not long departed hunter-gatherers could be seen returning with arms full of long, sturdy sticks and medium-sized, flat-bottomed, half house bricks. The boys proceeded to erect the pallets exactly as planned, banging sticks into the ground and standing the pallets upright against them, with the unbroken top sides facing inwards to create two flattish internal walls. Realising they would only need five pallets (three for mill side wall but only two for the Trinity side wall, leaving an entrance close to the tree and adjacent upright post), they broke the most badly damaged pallet up into bits and used the pieces for further vertical support. They removed the existing bricks from the roof, laid carefully ripped lengths of polythene carpet sleeves in an overlapping linear arrangement on top of the cardboard (being careful to offset the cardboard joints and the polythene joints), replaced the bricks, and added most of the extra ones brought back from the Wasteland. Then they broke any loose, hanging branches and twigs from the non-path side of the line of bushes, being careful not to damage the lovingly manicured shape of the park facing side, and stuffed the twigs into any available gaps in the pallet walls, securing the branches on the roof using the remaining half bricks.

The den was complete. Its camouflaging served only to make it more visible and obvious, at least from close range. Si ventured inside to discover last night's candles already lit, their stone bases arranged thoughtfully in a rough diamond pattern. They had been sensibly positioned in the corner diagonally opposite the door, allowing for a quick exit should an accident occur. Jay had made bunting with the fabric samples he had brought back from yesterday's trip to the moor, tying each piece to the next at the corners and tying the end and middle pieces to the frame of the pallets. Little Jay was sitting on his upturned crate and seemed proud that he had gathered the solitary piece of furniture. The carpet was dry, though, and would stay dry now that they had sorted the roof, so they wouldn't need any more seats.

To Si's amazement, Jules entered with a tape recorder, tapes and batteries. Straining his eyes in the half-light of the candles, Si counted everyone as now present. The others greeted the arrival of the music with the muted enthusiasm of those waiting in expectation, and Si felt hurt by not being party to the plan. He wondered if they'd made arrangements when he was out of earshot or, worse, if they'd deliberately decided he didn't need to be included. He decided they must have talked about it while they waited for him and Pete to turn up earlier, and felt better.

The song sounded good: the low roof, the insulated walls, the emptiness beyond the reach of the candles, the stillness, the carpet, the curtain of darkness that had fallen to cover the entrance. It all combined to give the music a low, deep, clear tone. Si felt an unfamiliar emotion forming behind his nose and at the back of his mouth. It felt great! It wasn't happiness or pride or good fortune or friendship. It was a special feeling. It was like importance and belonging and passion for the things he loved, all tangled in a knot that grew tighter and more confused behind his eyes. He felt the beginnings of tears and fought to stop them fully forming, leaning back against the Trinity side rear wall to hide his face from the candlelight.

The boys sat listening quietly for ages – perhaps fifteen minutes or more. They wallowed in the collective triumph of and shared pride in their new creation, though they all agreed that the rear walls needed some kind of covering, perhaps more cardboard. As the end of the tape drew tight against the full, right-hand spool, however, the boys began to shuffle and twitch and change position. Realising it was time to move on, Jules blew out the candles. The boys temporarily resumed their previous sitting positions to inhale the sweet smoke of the extinguished wicks while it lasted, the darkness enhancing their enjoyment and sense of smell. Si listened to the exaggerated deep nasal breaths, trying to identify the owner, which he was sure he could, though of course, he said nothing. Under the low roof, the acidic aftertaste of the flames hung stubbornly in the stagnant air, though the boys slowly tired of it and were soon assembled on the path beyond the neighbouring line of bushes.

It was a starry night. Jules had turned the tape over and was resting the tape recorder on his lower right arm, his hand stretching strategically through the space between the controls and the extending handle, his four fingers poised and ready on the four main controls: play, fast forward, rewind, stop. The magic of the music still held firm, though it was a different kind of magic – more rebellious, more joyous, more carefree. With heads bowed and nodding in worship, the group headed intuitively for the estate road.

Si felt fearsome and free. He loved the mystery of the night and the majesty of the stars and the music of footsteps on tarmac. It was a special moment. His lungs filled with an intense air of belonging. He felt at home in the moment, more than he ever had in the house, or at school, or during the daytime. He wanted the feeling to last forever — not the music or the memory; just the feeling.

Suddenly, Jay and Little Jay darted behind the path-side bushes, crouching down under the cover of the rhododendrons. Curious, the other boys peered over, perplexed.

"Police car!" warned Jay, nodding in the direction of the newsagents.

The other boys joined the brothers in the shelter of the shadows.

"It might have been the fence guy," Jase suggested.

"Yeah. I saw him heading towards the lights earlier," lied Pete. "I bet he was going to the box next to the hairdressers."

Si could see two policemen sitting in the front seats. He knew they weren't looking for the boys, as the car had its inside lights on, and the policemen would be sitting in darkness if they wanted to see out clearly. He also knew that nobody had called the police, as they would be sure to get an earful for wasting police time over a few broken pallets if they did. Si liked to play along, though. He enjoyed the pretend fear, the make-believe threat of pursuit, and the made-up sense of drama. He liked the feeling of togetherness, the sense of shared danger, the thought that they were all equally guilty. They were renegades, outlaws, bandits. Even if only for a few seconds.

The boys sat motionless and in complete silence for almost a minute. Si could smell the earth beneath his rubber soles. It smelt dirty and cold. It was dry, but the memory of the morning rain still lingered just beneath the surface. He pulled a leaf against his upper lip to block out the stench of the disturbed soil. It smelt clean and green, like lime juice. He rummaged in the darkness for a stone to sit on, as he knew they would have to remain hidden until the police car drove off, for nobody would want to acknowledge the pretence. To his sheer delight, he found an entirely whole and undamaged house brick.

He sat on the brick with his back against the low park wall. To his dismay, he realised that, of all seven boys, he was positioned furthest away from the lights of the estate road, and so his was the best and darkest hiding place. To his left, under the eaves of the bushes, an ominous void stretched back towards the clearing beside the playground. He suddenly felt uneasy and began to fidget. His biggest fear was of emptiness, of nothingness, of the absence of something, of something being missing. He tried to imagine what might be there. He imagined vampires, werewolves, ghosts, murderers, enemy soldiers. He felt better, as he knew that none of those things were really there, but then he felt worse, as he was faced again with the unknown. He decided to join in the conversation as, although he knew it was all nonsense, he needed the distraction.

"Maybe they're just checking the Wasteland, and then they'll move on," he suggested, knowing it to be untrue. He could see the policemen engrossed, reading something.

Moments later, the driver turned off the inside light, and the car pulled away in the direction of the crossroads. Si was the first to come out of hiding, feeling increasingly aware of his vulnerability to whatever wasn't there to his left. He headed at speed for the estate road, knowing the others would follow, desperate for the safety of the streetlights.

The boys didn't know what to do next, so they sought refuge under the halo of their favourite lamppost. Nobody spoke. Si was beginning to tire of the holiday and was looking forward to some bits of going back to school. He'd see lots of mates that he only ever saw on school days, and he'd have a school dinner every day, and he'd have a laugh in the corridors at swap over, and he'd play eleven-a-side at lunchtime, and some of the lessons were alright, and it wouldn't be too long until the camping trip, and there'd be matches after school until the clocks went back, and he'd get 40p every day for his dinner but he'd save some every day for the weekend, and then there'd be English with Mr Wildman. Best of all, though, he'd get to walk home with his mates every day. They would walk home different ways, and call off at different shops, and call in at each other's houses, and always be on the look-out for Westies or anyone from Trinity, and soon they would start collecting wood, and if they found anything they would pass the Wasteland on the way home so they could hide it there, and they could try to beat the bus, and sometimes they would. He still dreaded Sunday evening, but not Monday morning. Suddenly, he felt a desperate urgency to make the most of the remaining days.

"Let's go on the bikes tomorrow," he suggested.

"Yeah," agreed Jase. "Because the day after is Thursday, then it's Friday, then it's Saturday, then it's Sunday!"

Matty and Pete started to laugh. Jules followed suit, and soon, they were all laughing uncontrollably. Si struggled for air, for as soon as he caught a breath, it was gone again. His eyes felt warm, bathed in the blanket of tears welling under the cover of his closed eyelids. He began to cough and splutter, pressing the palm of his right hand against his chest in the hope of relief. He felt like he was choking or being strangled in a play fight. It felt brilliant!

"Then it's Monday," Jay added, and it started again from the beginning.

"Then it's Tuesday," said Matty. That was one too many, and it began to subside.

"I just meant that Matty and Pete won't be here on Thursday and I won't be here on Friday and Saturday is the trip and Sunday we won't be allowed!" Jase confirmed.

Impressed, everyone agreed, and a one o'clock departure time was quickly negotiated.

"Simon! Simon!"

Si was relieved to hear his dad calling him in from the side door step, as he was getting a bit bored and was looking forward to spending some time on his own. He ran back to the house, speeding up imperceptibly as he approached the alley that led to the school playing fields, and rushed back into the house through the door that his dad had left open for him. He grabbed five digestives from the packet in his favourite kitchen cupboard, filled a cup with milk from the fridge, peeked nervously into the living room to see who was sitting in their places, then walked in confidently and with disguised excitement as just his dad was in position.

"Where's Shaun and Mum?" Si asked.

"Shaun's out, Mum's in the bath," his dad replied.

"Bought some flights from Marsdens today, Dad," Si boasted.

"Good lad," his dad said. "I like it when you buy something useful with your money. People don't give it you to waste it on rubbish. I hate it when you buy those cards."

His dad was watching a movie which was set on a ship. Si couldn't immediately identify the type of ship, like he usually could, as it wasn't a cruise ship or a fishing boat or a naval vessel or an oil tanker or a container ship. It was a curious size, too. Kind of mid-sized. It was clearly a commercial vessel of some kind, though. Maybe some kind of support vessel? Si enjoyed watching it glide into the harbour. He liked to read the names on the containers stacked high in the background, too. They seemed oddly glamourous and sophisticated. He liked the cranes, the branded trucks and the dockside warehouses. He sometimes thought that he'd like to work on the docks when he grew up. It seemed like somewhere where important things got done, where people helped to keep things running and where you would do a lot of interesting jobs. He suspected from the colourisation of the film that the harbour wasn't in America. Maybe it was Mexico or Spain.

"Where's that, Dad?" Si asked.

"Greece," his dad replied.

Though he was wrong, Si was happy with his guess, and sat back to watch the rest of the movie. In a couple of minutes, though, the credits began to roll (he should have guessed from the ship entering the harbour). He decided to go upstairs.

His bedroom felt unusually cool and fresh, and he could feel the longer nights looming. He felt like he was standing in a shadow: the shadow of summer – growing taller, getting darker, gradually less distinct. He closed his bedroom window and looked out onto the estate. The streetlights lining the estate road shone like miniature exploding suns, the outer limits of their immediate reach blurred and indistinct as if shrouded in fog. He nine-tenths closed his eyes to exaggerate the force of the explosions. He could see supernovae, or castles burning on the horizon, or a row of amusements along the seafront. He closed his eyelids to watch what was happening inside, and to see what he could see when he couldn't see anything. It was pitch black and brilliant white, not in succession, but at the same time. Then it was mud orange, like the empty space between the leftover light from earth's surface and the blackness of the clear night sky above. He enjoyed not seeing, but he needed some music to make up the shortfall.

The opening bars of Track Six (Side Two, Track One)

took the edge off the unnerving, claustrophobic chill that hung heavy in the air. Si returned to the window, so that by looking out, he could concentrate on the music (he knew enough to know that the band were American – from New York). The streetlights at either side of the estate road lit the way to the park, forming an arrowhead as they met at the Wasteland crossroads.

Si felt like he was being tempted, taunted, mocked. Like he was being shown the way to a better, more exciting, more dynamic world, where life had more meaning, was fuller, wasn't wasted. He closed his eyes again. He imagined sitting on the back seat of a coach, nestled in the corner, looking out of a different window. The light was soft and easy on the eyes. A seemingly endless stream of semi-derelict, flat-roofed, open-doored buildings passed by below, beyond the barriers of the elevated highway. A frozen horizon of snow-clad skyscrapers loomed tall in the distance, their ice-glazed western faces twinkling like crystal as the setting sun crashed and burned on randomly scattered glacial shards. Surrounding the city, a barren scrubland looked on, unimpressed. Si imagined he was listening through headphones, and tilted his head a little to the left to enhance the stereo effect of the speakers. The vision projected onto the silver screen behind his eyelids was full of romance, brimming with adventure, fraught with danger. Si soaked up the music, which he could feel burning inside him. He felt a crippling sense of longing, of urgency, of missed opportunity. He could feel tears welling just below his top lashes again.

He opened his eyes. The streetlights were like smashed Christmas tree stars, draped in smudged silver tinsel. Everything else was blurred and indistinct, except the music, which was fresh and clean and clear and precise. He fought to keep the tears in. It wasn't too hard, as they weren't the proper tears of sadness or pain or joy, but the half tears of mixed, confused emotions. He felt alive. He was a little bit happy and a little bit sad and a little bit inspired and a little bit frustrated – but a lot alive.

He listened to the rest of Side Two, holding his position at the window after Track Ten to enjoy the sound of the needle clicking hypnotically every other second (for longer than was probably wise). Resigned to calling it a day, he lurched slowly into the bathroom. He completed his bedtime routine in record time and was laid in bed within a minute. He decided not to read his book, or memorise the stats on some of his football cards, or count his money, or write in his notebook, as he was utterly exhausted. He fell asleep with the memory of a smile on his face, as in the dying moments of the day, he remembered that he still had 85p in treat money.

4

The Twinkling Stars

Si woke to the burning glare of the sun, as he'd forgotten to close his curtains before getting into bed. He jumped up to shut out the light, then rushed back to the safety of the sheets. He loved to sit in his room with the curtains drawn, especially in bright sunlight. He felt like he was in his own private world: hidden from prying eyes, forgotten and neglected, left to fend for himself. He had a strong sense of being alone – not scared or lonely, but brave, independent, resourceful, adventurous. He thought about the things he would have to do for himself until his mum got home: making breakfast, confirming arrangements with Brian, locking the door, getting some dinner, tidying the garage. He'd got used to doing all these things over the course of the holiday, but this was the first time that he'd thought about it.

He decided to start the day later, as he was enjoying the secret satisfaction of his solitude. The light was soft and calming and, unlike darkness, made Si feel sleepy. He closed his eyes to listen to the house, though he knew he was home alone. He could hear the bricks in the wall settling into place, and the glass in the window frame adjusting position, and the floorboards creaking under the weight of daytime ghosts. He could hear the water in the pipes and the smoke in the chimney and gas escaping from the cooker. He turned down the inside and turned up the outside. He could hear a low, guttural, rumbling sound. It was barely audible, indecipherable. Maybe it was distant traffic thundering through the lights, or the wind dancing around the chimney stacks, or a train rattling across the moor. Or maybe he was imagining it. He sat motionless so as to listen carefully, but he could only hear better, not more clearly. It was the sound of mid-morning, of the quiet time between breakfast and dinner. It was the sound of nothing happening.

After an indeterminable length of time with his hands behind his head – staring at the ceiling, his body clock slowed, stuttered, stopped – he decided to go downstairs to make breakfast.

On the kitchen table, some mystery items lay hidden under the tea towel. On top of the tea towel sat a hastily written note which read 'Touch these and your dead!' Si removed the tea towel to discover two jam sandwiches and a mug of milk. He laughed, as he knew Shaun had made them for him, just so that he could leave him a note which read 'Touch these and your dead!'

He took his milk and sandwiches into the living room, flicked the switch on the socket on the stairs-side wall, and settled down in front of the TV. The test card came on. The TV was on 2. As it was the school holidays, he knew there would be kids' TV on 1. He was busy with his sandwiches, though, so he left the channel unchanged for a few minutes. He thought he could see slight, sudden, irregular movements along the borders between the shaded shapes, amongst the blocks of parallel lines, and along the lines of blackboard chalk. When he concentrated, though, all movement at the focal point stopped, only to be exaggerated in other areas of his peripheral view. He focussed on different areas of the card, but the moving parts merely seemed to shift around the screen, deliberately avoiding detection. He turned the TV onto 1 with his big toe.

On 1 was a programme about making things, which he never did, so he flicked the socket switch off, again with his big toe. He took his plate and mug into the kitchen and did the washing up. He made a cup of tea and returned to the living room to enjoy the luxury of his dad's chair again. He knew there would only be a few more mornings between now and the half-term holiday that he would be able to get away with it, so he would make the most of it.

Noise from outside drew him to the window. The street was busier now, with children playing and cars going by and mums chatting in gardens and dogs sniffing at gate posts and the insurance man knocking at number 22 and cats finding shady spots and Pete riding up and down on his bike, practising braking with the soles of his trainers. Si didn't feel part of it. He couldn't shake the feeling of being alone, of not being included, of watching from afar, of being outside it all. He decided not to waste any more of what was left of the holiday looking out of windows, as it always made him feel isolated and regretful.

He realised that, having used up much of his staying-in allowance the previous day, he couldn't avoid going out for much longer, so he finished his cup of tea and climbed upstairs to begin his morning routine.

Five minutes later, he was on the dividing wall looking over the dividing fence, having locked the door and hidden the key under the plant pot next to the drain.

"Brian! Brian!" he called.

"Who goes there?" came a reply from upstairs.

"We're going on the bikes."

"Right-o! Take some two pence pieces from my jar, just in case. And stay together!"

"Will do times two. Thanks!"

Si jumped over the fence, opened the kitchen door, and took 10p in twos from the jar on top of the fridge. He closed the kitchen door, jumped back over the fence, and headed straight for the garage, opening the door with his customary care and precision. He rolled his bike out into the light of the drive and dropped it unceremoniously onto the crumbling tarmac. He returned to the garage door, which he closed with even greater attention to detail, as the horizontal to vertical manoeuvre was always the trickiest. He got on his bike and rode out into the street with the usual level of swagger and confidence, opening up his imaginary throttle to let more imaginary petrol into his imaginary engine.

He rode up to Pete and cut straight to business, as morning greetings were superfluous. "You wanna put a cable on?" asked Si.

"Yeah!" Pete replied.

Si rode back onto the drive, jumping off his bike before it had stopped moving in a forced display of urgency. Pete was standing astride his bike on the pavement, supported by a gatepost, showing the expected level of respect for and fear of someone else's property. Si signalled for him to cross the threshold as he lifted the garage door overhead, and Pete rode hurriedly into the semi-darkness, braking with the thinning soles of his trainers. Taking one of the cables that he'd liberated from Brian's bikes the day before, Si quickly threaded the business end of the cable through the slot in Pete's back brake lever so that the head sat snugly in position. Then he threaded the casing through the eyelets on the frame, loosened the holding nut on the rear calliper with his multi-tool, threaded the uncased bare back end of the cable through the hole in the anchor bolt, pulled the cable tight with some pliers, and retightened the holding nut. He tested the brake. It was a bit keen, but he knew that it would loosen up during the afternoon, plus the pads would wear away a bit. At the moment, they were as good as new, unlike Pete's trainers.

"Be careful at first, until you get used to it," Si warned.

"OK," Pete replied.

Si cleared up, as he'd left a few things out and lying around the previous day. He enjoyed tidying the garage, knowing his dad liked everything neatly arranged and returned to its allocated place. The garage was a special place that Si and his dad shared and maintained together, as nobody else ever entered. He decided that later he would tell his dad he'd been working in the garage, knowing he would approve and be suitably impressed. More than anything, he feared his dad's disapproval.

Having completed his tidying routine to the usual high standard, Si lowered the garage door with meticulous care and attention to detail so as not to misalign anything within the neat rows of tools, brushes and pencils on the worktops. Pete was already riding backwards and forwards and in unconvincing circles in front of the house, testing his back brake every few yards. Si rolled out of the drive, stopping in the centre of Pete's unconvincing circles. Pete rode round a few times until he had remastered the technique. When comfortable with his handling, and having built up a smooth and steady motion, he risked riding single-handed, twirling his free hand in theatrical little circles, mimicking a cowboy circling an unsuspecting bull with lasso primed and ready. Si recognised this as a challenge and resolved to break his record for riding hands-free at some time in the afternoon (he claimed that his record was ten seconds, but in reality, it was more like five or maybe six seconds).

Unexpectedly, Pete mounted the kerb and headed off along the pavement in the direction of the park and the Wasteland. Si thought this a bit premature, as they weren't due to assemble until one o'clock. He realised he had neglected his usual awareness of the time (sometimes intuitive, sometimes conscious) and glanced at his watch. It was half past eleven. He took off his watch and rubbed the back against the right leg of his jeans, then he rubbed the front and back of the pale, sun-starved wrist of his left arm on the left leg of his jeans, as he'd had his watch on continuously since having a bath on Saturday and both watch and wrist were sticky with sweat and congealed dirt. He put his watch back on and walked his bike up onto the kerb, mounted carefully, and rode slowly and cautiously along the uneven but mercifully traffic-free pavement, following Pete from a respectful distance. He decided that they should get something to eat before departing for the afternoon, and that he would pay for Pete, as long as the others didn't arrive first. He smiled, then laughed, then shrieked in delight as he remembered he had an unprecedented 95p in food and treat money. Rising from the saddle, he swung his bike to and fro, stamping on the peddles in an unconscious, reflex reaction to the sheer elation, and soon caught up.

Pete stopped and dismounted at the newsagents and propped his bike carefully against the graffiti-splattered sidewall. Si followed suit, and they both went inside, the bell above the door heralding their entrance. The newsagents was more old-fashioned than the shop, and had less of almost everything, and shut at six o'clock Monday to Saturday and twelve on Sunday. Its main attraction was the glass cabinet of sandwiches and cakes. Si was having second thoughts about his recent uncharacteristic rush of generous intentions, as Pete obviously had some money. Pete bought two packets of crisps and a can of pop, so he obviously didn't have much.

"You wanna sarny or a cake?" Si asked, a little reluctantly.

After a long selection process, Pete chose to have the potted meat, so Si bought a corned beef and a potted meat sandwich, a currant slice (there was only one currant slice left, and it was a big one, so he'd be sure to get it) and a can of pop. 38p. He figured that, because he'd bought Pete a sandwich, and if he gave him a quarter of his currant slice too, he'd be sure to get a packet of crisps in return. That way, he would have been kind, but not too kind. It didn't do to be too kind. It made the recipient feel uncomfortable and suspicious and confused and unworthy. A little gesture to a friend was OK, though, as long as it remained a secret, and as long as there was no-one else around to mock or abuse or complain or, worst of all, to feel slighted or inferior to others.

Pete closed the door behind him, the ring of the bell tolling a muffled farewell. The boys pushed their bikes over to a bare patch in the middle of the Wasteland and laid them down on the weed-ridden rubble to eat. Si placed his bike down carefully, as he had his new grips on, and he didn't want to scuff the ends. They each made a seat from a section of the same broken paving stone, then shared their purchases according to the unwritten code of rights and wrongs which governed such arrangements. Pete responded instinctively to his friend's unprompted act of kindness, and Si ate his crisps first. They each opened their cans of pop, placing both centrally so they could share without the need to ask. They each offered their half-eaten sandwiches to the other, though neither was allowed to accept. Si offered Pete a bit of his currant slice, which was gratefully accepted, though a second piece was naturally refused.

The roads were unusually quiet, and the park was deserted. There was no weather, just a featureless white sky where the weather should be. There was nearly an hour to kill, which wasn't long enough to be productively engaged, so the boys occupied themselves with the usual pointless pursuits. They threw stones at their empty pop cans. They searched the weeds for wood, hiding each piece in the tall grass near the newsagents. They looked for discarded bottles, agreeing beforehand to sort their discoveries into separate piles for returners, keepers and targets, though they found none. They searched for anything, everything, something. Si found a fork and a spoon in the undergrowth and decided to store them with the rest of his bike tools in the only drawer that his dad said he was allowed to use. With this small victory, the search was called off, and the two friends could relax.

They returned to their respective pieces of paving and sat in silence. Si's thoughts returned to the start of the new school year. He felt a faint but growing sense of panic in his lungs and across his chest. His lungs didn't feel full or empty or hot or cold, and his chest didn't feel tight or weak or puffed or sunken. He just felt aware of them. He could just feel them when normally they went unnoticed for months. He took some exaggerated deep breaths and the feeling dissolved, like sugar in hot milk.

Jules, Matty and Jase arrived on their bikes, instinctively falling into a circular procession, surrounding Pete and Si like seagulls hovering over discarded promenade scraps. Si could see that they were concentrating hard and holding on tight and balancing carefully, each of their faces flushed in an effort not to lose ground by stopping, though the surface was obviously too uneven for showing off. Jay and Little Jay were absent, as Si had suspected they would be, as Little Jay was probably a bit too young for this adventure, and Jay had probably stayed at home in sympathy (or been told to).

Si and Pete got on their bikes as Jules led the way to the favoured place to cross the park road, which was directly in front of the newsagents' front window, and boasted sunken kerbs on either side and a good view in both directions. Jules waited patiently, not just until no cars could be seen on the road, but until none could be heard approaching, as he knew that they would have to cross separately, and that from the point at which he rose unannounced to swagger across, it would be at least ten seconds until the last bike mounted the far pavement. Upon reaching the other side, Jules stopped and watched and waited for the last boy to arrive unharmed, assuming responsibility for the group and concerned for everyone's safety.

When everyone was safely across, Jules resumed his leadership role and rode along the pavement in the direction of the street that led to the main entrance to the carpet place. He waited again at the turning, as they were heading onto quieter streets and would ride on the road from now on. When all had reassembled, he led the way off the kerb, over the white line, and onto the left-hand side of the road.

The road swept gently downhill as the boys freewheeled joyfully past the entrance to the access road that led to the carpet place. They passed the house of the unofficial guardian of the carpet place courtyard, who could be seen removing garden tools and weedkiller from the requisitioned coal bunker at the side of the house. In one of those extraordinary, mind-blowing coincidences that happens every few days, his entire body was visible, but not his head, which was buried deep amongst the half-empty paint tins and emergency plant pots in one of the damp, spider-infested corners. Jules turned right into semi-familiar territory. Si began to lift his right arm to signal until, realising his mistake, he quickly withdrew it to the safety of his new grips.

The mood in the group shifted as they turned left onto the vaguely familiar hospital approach road. They were in largely unchartered waters now, so rode more slowly and with due respect to what might be lurking beneath. Si felt reckless and irresponsible, something he hated to experience alone, but which felt good within his band of untamed renegades. He imagined being watched through twitching lace curtains, his every move followed as the reflector on his rear mudguard disappeared slowly out of range, suspicious eyes tracking his steady retreat to a safe distance, Venetian blinds being opened slowly and surreptitiously to maintain one-way observation of his leisurely departure. He knew really, though, that nobody had even noticed their presence.

Jules sped up as they entered the hospital grounds, as technically they weren't allowed to ride through there. Within a minute, though, they had exited triumphantly through the archway at the main entrance. The sun had come out, the morning's cover of featureless blanket cloud torn asunder by an unforgiving August sun.

Jules stopped to draw breath in the shallow shadow of the hospital wall, the other boys following suit obediently. Si looked up to inspect the sky, stepping out of the shade to check the angle and length of his shadow, making his daily observations of the speed and direction of the wind. Satisfied with the accuracy of his analysis, he gratefully accepted a swig from the bottle of cream soda that Matty had brought along for the ride. It was a home delivery bottle, a little narrower than a shop-bought deposit bottle, and Matty had just about managed to force it into his cage.

Jase assumed leadership for the next leg of the journey, heading straight for one of the several local networks of streets referred to as 'the new estate' (mostly by adults). The pace picked up a little as Jase attempted to show his worth by breaking away from the pack, by cornering confidently, by pretending to know where he was going, and by forcing the first split in the group.

There was no sense of direction to the route, no due caution, no final destination, no given purpose, and Si was beginning to worry. Matty forced his way to the front and, having assumed leadership at speed, had nowhere to go but faster, farther. Unfamiliar vistas opened up around every corner, the route lined with mysterious porches, curious brickwork, strange driveways and peculiar fencing. Si kept an eye out for street signs, for although he had long since been comfortable with his surroundings, he still half-recognised many of the names, probably from half-listening to his mum and dad's half-hearted plans to move house: Windermere Road, Coniston Avenue, Grasmere Drive. Upon turning onto Blenheim Grove, however, all sense of recognition evaporated, and he was glad to see Pete taking up the reins, as he knew this would signal a return to normality.

Pete rocked listlessly from one pedal to the other in a slow, languid, indifferent rhythm, displaying admirable confidence and assurance, leading the group assertively in the search for a suitable resting place. The boys all glanced from side to side, checked the road behind, surveyed the route ahead. They assumed an exaggerated air of caution, like the sepia outlaws of Saturday movies riding into hostile territory. The streets were deserted, the soaring heat drawing sticky black lava from the fault lines in the tarmac, sending the less committed scurrying for the safety of the shade. Pete spotted the perfect pitstop, an empty stretch of greenery at the junction of two unremarkable estate roads, one of the dozens of pointless patches of grass that punctuated the town's estates. He jumped the kerb and led the group across the pavement, semi-dismounting and rolling to a stop with both feet on his right pedal. He collapsed to the ground in feigned exhaustion suitably close to the reassurance of the road, as everybody hated riding on grass.

Everyone drank a carefully measured fifth of the remnants of the cream soda, the normal rules of ownership and distribution abandoned as Matty declined to take the lion's share. Si could detect the disguised anxiety in his mates' faces. It was clear that no-one had a clear grip on their whereabouts. He was confident he could lead them safely home, though. He had noticed that, up until now, they had mostly had the wind at their backs, as they had chased cloud shadows along the faster stretches, overtaking as they returned victorious into the blinding light of early afternoon. He also knew that they were now significantly further to the east, as he had traced the arc of the sun across the sky, and was sure they could retrace their route using the slowly setting sun as their guiding star. He was also aware that they had lost a lot of height. If they rode uphill, into the wind, with the sun on their faces, then at the very least, they would soon return to familiar territory and be able to plot the remainder of the return leg comfortably. He decided to say nothing but to assume the lead at the appropriate time.

As all his mates were laid on their backs, hands behind their heads, eyes closed, chewing grass, Si decided to survey his surroundings for future reference. Although he was certain that he had never been there before, everything looked tired and familiar: the pebble-dashed panels of the easy-assemble garages, the decorative stones adorning the dividing walls, the multi-coloured strip blinds hanging from every open side door. He was lost and anxious and longed to return to safer streets, though he still felt a pang of sadness at the mournful sight of the all too familiar.

Unannounced, Si stood, mounted his bike, and rode to the kerbside to await the others, indicating his intention to lead. The rest followed leisurely but dutifully, and they were soon headed for home with Si at the front of the pack. He loosely followed his three-point plan of action, carefully combined with an attempt at visual recognition, which was always difficult in the opposite direction, and soon they were within sight of the main hospital building. Upon glancing back, however, he noticed they were being followed. A boy and a girl hung behind at a relatively safe but menacing distance, standing on the pedals as if poised for pursuit. Si nodded in their direction to alert the others, and they all looked back in perfect unison, as if posing for a photograph.

Jase led the escape, swinging his bike from side to side with well-practised precision. They had barely seen a moving car all afternoon, and the roads were blissfully quiet, so Pete swung to the right-hand side of the road and powered through to the front of the pack, taking his turn to bear the brunt of the wind. Si looked nervously across, as he hardly ever broke the Highway Code, but seeing that the road ahead was clear, he swung over into Pete's slipstream. Further over to the right, the Queen Elizabeth Wing flashed in and out of sight through the gaps between the semis, the top two floors visible above the back yard fences. Si forced his way to the front, turning first right with the quiet satisfaction that he had led them back to the relative safety of the hospital.

Part of the archway at the main entrance could be seen between the gaps in the unkempt hedge of a school football field. Instinctively, the pace began to ease, the sight of the familiar fraying the edge of fear, like the face of a friend amongst the uniforms of a rival school. Si looked back to see the chasing duo speed straight past the right hand turning, knowing that they'd never had any intention of following. Now was the perfect opportunity. Si rode with uncharacteristic concentration, attentive to the delicate relationship between power, balance and speed, maintaining a straight line with fingertips feathering the grips. He rested his arms by his side and began to count: one, two, three, four, five, six, seven, eight, nine. He was happy with that, especially as the others were all behind him, and couldn't help but see.

Si led the way through the archway, the pack regrouping for the short sprint along the forbidden arteries of the hospital grounds, maintaining safety in numbers. They were soon back within the comforting arms of legal road use, and began the long climb back up to the park road.

Si remained seated, trying not to show the strain, but he was beginning to tire. Nobody spoke. Every stream of thought and suggestion and ill-advised question evaporated in the sweltering heat of the dead of the afternoon like summer raindrops on sun-baked flagstones. Si chose a succession of visual targets, breaking the climb down into more easily digestible chunks: a blue Cortina, a white Allegro, a telegraph pole with a length of bunting hanging loose, the shortcut to the carpet place, a yellow Capri, the guardian's garden. One final push and the pack were riding the crest of the park road, an oasis of lengthening grass in the centre of an unofficial football pitch drawing them over like a cowboy movie mirage.

They couldn't be bothered to ride to the safe crossing place, so they pushed their bikes across the road and straight through the dog walkers' entrance, collapsing onto the cool, soft bed of the unmarked centre circle. Si still had 57p, so he offered to buy a bottle of pop if someone else would go to the newsagents for it. Pete agreed to do the honours, so Si gave him two ten pence pieces, leaving him two tens, a five and six twos.

As the others discussed their courageous escape from the imagined pursuit, Si's thoughts turned to Shaun, as they often did when he was sitting on the grass in the park. He remembered when he was allowed to join in when Shaun and his mates were playing cricket, and how he made a sliding block to stop the ball from reaching the tarmac of the boundary path. He remembered that time on the putting green, when

Shaun decided they would play each hole twice to make the game last longer. He remembered how they used to play bowls, taking it very seriously, and how Shaun explained the rules and tactics. He remembered their games of tennis, when Shaun would play left-handed for a bit to make the score more even, though never for long enough to lose. More memories trickled out from deep inside, from forgotten corners, from a lifetime ago. He felt sad and lonely and a hundred years old. Pete returned with the bottle of pop, so Si filled the empty spaces with carbon dioxide, drowning his sorrows in shandy.

The rest of the afternoon was wasted riding pointless circuits of the park perimeter, stopping for unnecessary rest breaks and taking half-hearted turns on the swings, slide and see-saw. Familiarity began to breed contempt within the group, and slowly the pack began to thin as boys broke off to pursue their own interests, eventually leaving each to his own.

The day had begun its steady descent, so Si closed his eyes and turned his face to the slowly fading light. The power of the sun was still savage and untamed, though the summer holidays had taken the edge off its unforgiving sting. At the height of the day, Si rarely sought the solace of the shade, only reluctantly sheltered from the heat, and regularly suffered the consequences of overexposure. When darkness fell and the gentle summer night breezes licked his face and forearms, he often endured the memory of the day. At this moment, though, he basked in the glory. The heat was tender, and the light was muted, and this was the best time of the day and the best day of the week and the best week of the year and the best year of his life, but soon it would be all forgotten.

In the middle of the football field, around the non-existent centre spot, he rode his bike in dizzying Spirograph circles to survey the scene. All his mates had disappeared. Safe in the knowledge that they would be certain to reconvene later with the same unspoken, casual rudeness, he headed for home.

Not knowing whether or not he would need it later, Si propped his bike up against the garage door. The rest of the family were sitting on the front lawn, his mum and dad on deckchairs and Shaun on the garden blanket. A makeshift picnic was laid out on rain-starved grass, the plates strategically positioned on the bald patches. Si laid down next to Shaun on the blanket and helped himself to a corned beef sandwich, a packet of cheese and onion crisps and a mug of yellow lemonade.

"Where you been?" asked Shaun.

"The other side of the hospital," Si replied.

"It's a good bike, that is," his dad boasted. "Those gears are Italian. The saddle's one of the best you can get, too. Must have cost a fortune when it was brand new."

"I hope you're careful on that thing!" his mum added.

"Yeah," Si responded.

"It's been a funny day," said Dad. "It didn't know what to do earlier. It was sunny first thing, then it clouded over. Then it brightened up again, but now it's lovely!"

Si was familiar with Dad's regular summary of the day's weather. It was strangely reassuring, like being told where the races were on tomorrow, or what was doing well in the garden, or how many runs were needed. His dad was right, though: it was a perfect afternoon.

It had been a working day as usual for most of the adults on the estate, so many were sitting out to make the most of the rest of the day. The sun had begun to slowly withdraw, its face turning a deeper, richer, more tolerable shade as it slid slowly towards the roof tiles along Birch Avenue. Those sitting on the lucky side of the street raised their cheeks to acknowledge its gentle farewell. The air tried to circulate unnoticed through the open gates and around the back yards and over the dividing fences, though Si could feel its cool breath tickling the hairs on his arms. The shade grew deeper, darker and less welcoming, its reach crawling slowly across the street towards Si's favourite kerbstones. The fronts on the lucky side remained in mellow sunlight, though the glare on the windows softened steadily as the whole estate fell under the shadow of the day. Si listened to the distant song of contentment ebbing and flowing to the music of cutlery on china, of doors settling softly into their frames, of the strips of fly blinds dancing in the breeze, of kettles whistling in empty kitchens, of the faint hum of a lawnmower crawling habitually across unresponsive grass. He shuffled over onto the lawn, lying face down to luxuriate in the delicious scent of the soil. He closed his eyes.

Si woke with a start. Feeling cold and damp, he looked down at his chest and stomach to check for wet patches. To his amazement, he was bone dry. Everyone else had packed up and headed inside, leaving only the garden blanket. He rolled over and stared up at the cloudless sky. The spaces between the wisps of his fringe were a perfect pale blue. Closing one eye at a time, he analysed the colour of near space beyond each side of the tip of his nose. The light grew paler from right to left, confirming what he already knew about the position of the setting sun (when on holiday, or when anywhere unfamiliar, Si was always keen to trace the movement of the sun's path across the sky. Because of this, he always claimed to know which direction was north and was often tested). His face felt sticky and bloated, and he could feel the pitted pattern left by the grass on his right cheek and temple. He felt his forehead, which was less sore than expected and had a late summer texture: smooth, clear and fresh air-dried. He stood up, shook the garden blanket, folded it four times, and headed indoors.

The remainder of the makeshift picnic was laid on the kitchen table, awaiting his arrival. He had three more sandwiches (one corned beef and two jam), two more packets of crisps (both ready salted) and polished off the yellow lemonade, placing the bottle in the allocated space for empties at the side of the fridge. He was still hungry, so he made himself a sugar sandwich and grabbed the bourbons from his favourite kitchen cupboard. When he'd finally had enough, he staggered tiredly into the living room and crashed onto the sofa.

His dad was watching the news. Si never listened to the news, though he liked to watch the reports. Trucks sped along a desert road as a column of black smoke rose in the distance. A man on a rooftop spoke directly to the camera, the night lights of a faraway city twinkling at each side of his camouflage jacket. A woman in the back of a speeding car interrogated the anonymous driver, graffiti-clad buildings streaming past through the half-open window. Shoppers walked down the high street of an unfamiliar town. He closed his eyes again, not to sleep, but in the hope that the darkness might release the tension in his face, neck and shoulders. He took a few deep, exaggerated breaths, relishing the release of each exhalation, savouring the silence of the six seconds between each draw.

"We'll have to get what you need for next week on Saturday, I think," said Dad.

"OK. I don't need much," Si replied.

Reluctantly, and through fear of temporary excommunication, Si decided to head out again, despite the tiredness in his neck, shoulders and wrists. Bypassing his usual kitchen stop-off points, he ventured hesitantly back into the sun, which was now mercifully low and benign. His bike still stood propped up against the garage door, and he winced at the thought of the painful process required to store it securely within. He completed each manoeuvre with his customary attention to detail, though, feeling each creak and groan of the panels and wheels in his spine and hips.

He shuffled along the estate road towards the park and Wasteland, stopping at every given opportunity. He sat for a while on one of the denim-polished stones along a familiar stretch of wall, next to one of the several assembly point lampposts where he knew he wouldn't attract unwarranted attention. Pulling a stubborn shard of gravel from one of the time-worn holes at the heel of his right sole, he sluggishly scratched his initials next to the more permanent, weather-beaten carvings of boys long grown.

Farther on, he sat for a while at a respectful distance

from a group of younger children playing in the street. Settling on an unoccupied length of concrete kerbstone, he observed from a position sufficiently removed to indicate that he just wanted to watch and not to join in. An empty beer can stood upright in the middle of the road. Two boys were leaning on a low garden wall whilst a third searched frantically behind the bins and in the bushes of the gardens nearby. Suddenly, a girl jumped up from behind a disused coal bunker and darted in delight towards the street. The seeker followed suit as the two prisoners stood poised for escape. A car approached from the park end of the road, and all four players simultaneously groaned in bitter disappointment. A fifth player appeared from behind a tree and walked calmly into the street to remove the offending can. Si watched as the car crawled past and trundled slowly towards The Birches, interrupting proceedings at several points along the way.

Farther on, he sat for a while on the grass verge that adorned the roadside at the entrance to the estate, watching the cars approach from different directions. Someone waved whilst driving carefully past, but Si didn't realise who it was until he read the rear number plate. He instantly felt guilty and disrespectful and vowed to make it up to Brian at the first chance. He turned again to face the infrequent oncoming traffic and saw Jules approaching along the pavement.

"I'm going to the old chapel. You wanna come?" asked Jules upon arrival.

"Yeah, OK," Si replied.

The old chapel was at the far side of the lights, next to the Sunday School. It was only a five-minute walk from the park, but it was in an area unfamiliar to Si. On his side of the main road, Si knew every shortcut, broken gate, forbidden entrance, unofficial path, loose fencing that you could crawl under and blunted barbed wire that you could climb over for miles around. On the other side of the main road, only a few hundred yards from his house, however, he once got lost whilst delivering a catalogue payment to the agent's house.

Suggesting a pit-stop at the shop at the lights, Si took the change from his money pocket to double-check, as he did several times every day. He decided to spend his copper and a five. He hadn't needed to make a phone call in the afternoon, so he still had the five twos from Brian's copper jar, plus an extra two from his change from the newsagents that morning. The top of his right thigh was sore from the constant rubbing, so he calculated that he could use seven of the coins, have only two left, but still spend less than half. He held 17p in his right hand and transferred two tens to his back left pocket.

"I'll get us something to take with us," Si confirmed, making it clear that he was willing to buy for both of them, as he knew that Jules wouldn't have any money on him, and that he was likely to try to help himself if a window of opportunity opened, especially as it was a shop in which they weren't well known. Si subtly suggested that Jules wait outside and was relieved when he reluctantly agreed. He had hoped that Jules would submit to the temporary seniority conferred upon him by virtue of his superior purchasing power but wasn't sure.

Si bought two packets of crisps, two rolls of toffees and two halfpenny chews, and shared them accordingly. They both ate the chew first, then the crisps, then a few toffees. Then they each stored the remainder of the toffees in their front right pocket. Si stopped at the bin outside the Sunday School to dispose of the empty crisp packet and toffee wrappers. Still under the spell of Si's momentary higher rank, Jules retraced his steps a few paces to pick up his crisp packet and did likewise.

The old chapel was accessed via a formerly lesser-used side entrance, hidden from the road along a dark, damp, overgrown path between the main building and the high stone wall of the neighbouring houses. The door was ajar, and Si pushed it open with ease, though Jules (for dramatic effect) climbed in through the empty space where the lower pane of a sash window used to be. The floor was strewn with broken glass and the wafer-thin pages of savaged hymn books, though the pews, altar and lectern were all largely untouched. Si recognised it immediately as the petty, affected vandalism of youthful, superficial criminality, too unconvincing and contrived to do lasting damage. The last light of the sun diffused solemnly through the remnants of a stained-glass window, casting ill-defined seeds of multi-coloured light amongst the long infertile benches and onto the barren, shattered floor tiles.

Si felt trapped, overcome by the sensation of someone looking in from outside. He couldn't see any purpose in their presence there, which only emphasised his growing anxiety. He wasn't a thief, and there was barely anything worth stealing anyway. He never broke things without good reason. There was nothing deserving of attention there, though he feigned interest in Jules's supposedly fascinating discoveries: more hymn books, lengths of cloth, discarded lead flashing. He began to suspect that Jules had suggested the visit merely to win the begrudging admiration of the other boys upon return. He felt resentful, and the discomfort intensified. He was gripped by a familiar sense of something being out of place, of something being inexplicably wrong, of something being upside down/inside out/back-to-front. Staring at the dark, abandoned cross within the sun-bleached panelling that long since held the crucifix, he was visited by the unwelcome, recurring images which haunted his daytime dreams: a wolf wandering the streets of the estate, a ship rusting at the bottom of the ocean, the skeletal hands of the arms that beckon from the darkness of the school playing fields.

"I'm going back to the shop," Si exclaimed, knowing it would give him ample justification for a hasty departure.

Within ten seconds, he was back on the pavement, walking in disguised terror towards the sanctuary of the traffic lights. Upon turning to re-enter the shop, he noticed Jules following at a dignified distance. He laughed out loud in disapproval, knowing that Jules had stayed on alone in the old chapel as long as he had dared (which wasn't long) to prove a point. He bought two cartons of blackcurrant juice for 5p each and exited on the double, Jules arriving with perfect timing to ungratefully accept his share as the lights turned to green, preventing crossing.

"Got a pin?" Si asked.

Jules delved into the left breast pocket of his denim jacket and fished out a badge. Pulling the pin out to an unnatural position, he pierced a hole in the outer edge of the plastic film at the top of each carton. Holding the carton in front of his face, Si squeezed to direct the stream of juice into his open mouth. Jules copied, holding the carton at twice the distance in an attempt to assume superiority. Si was annoyed, though both boys laughed as the juice dribbled down Jules's chin and onto his t-shirt, and all was forgotten.

The lights turned to red, and they crossed together, staring silently at each other with giggling eyes as they guzzled the juice from different heights and at contrasting speeds and various angles.

Upon reaching the boundary of home territory, marked by the path side park privets, both boys noticed their three co-adventurers swaying solemnly on the swings (Jay and Little Jay were still AWOL). Si waved in greeting, though it went unnoticed, and Jules gave a mocking chuckle. Si was beginning to tire of Jules's sneers, and was looking forward to reconvening with the others.

The five were reunited, though Si sensed a pensive, contemplative mood within the group. Everyone seemed tired: of each other, of the holiday, of the park, of the estate, of the relentless requirement to fill every precious hour with doing, trying, searching, partaking. Matty suggested sitting in the den, and nobody could be bothered to disagree. The den had temporarily lost its magic, the cold cardboard having lost its texture of reassurance, the walls and ceiling seeming more confined, the atmosphere claustrophobic. Si knew that the magic would return one day, conjured out of the thin summer air, but tonight it had evaporated, leaving just pallets and bricks, as conspicuous as a clumsy card trick.

Pete suggested splitting up to search for things, and nobody could be bothered to disagree. Si decided to walk the perimeter of the park, knowing the vacant space bordering the wall, fence and privets to be fertile scavenging ground, though on this occasion, he foraged with weary indifference. Normally he would search with an ardent curiosity (they rarely looked for anything specific, for how would you know what to look for, if you didn't know what you might find?), but tonight the lack of motive and purpose left him frustrated. He merely kicked around in the undergrowth, then picked up, inspected and discarded with disdain. Upon regrouping, the mood was lifted somewhat by Jase's discovery of a screwdriver, but in practical terms, the search had been fruitless.

Jules suggested climbing onto the roof of the park pavilion, and nobody could be bothered to disagree. Each boy scaled the façade by the same method: pile of bricks, windowsill, metal grille, gutter, right arm over, belly up, right leg over, press up, left leg over, stand up. The parkkeepers had protected the pavilion from break-ins by installing metal grilles over the windows, but these had merely provided useful hand and footholds, making the roof more easily accessible. All five boys lay in a neat row on the coarse, grasping, unforgiving safety of the bitumen felt, staring skywards. A long silence ensued, each boy seemingly lost in his own clumsy, ill-formed, profound thoughts. Pete decided to go for some chips and announced that he would get some for Si to partly repay his dinnertime debt. Jase, Jules and Matty followed Pete, Si agreeing to follow shortly.

Si lay back to survey the sky. Darkness had fallen halfway, and a scattering of stars came out one by one, rousing from their daytime slumber. The brightest hung low in the western sky, glistening gracefully through the slowly descending curtain of night, the last of the day bowing in acceptance beneath its ragged rim as it retired from the stage. Si wondered. If the Earth was a sphere, and if he occupied a point on an imaginary line of longitude circling the surface of the Earth, then he must be the closest person on Earth to whichever star occupied the end of an imaginary straight line drawn from the centre of the Earth that passed through his body before continuing out into space. The maths made sense, though like the sky above, it seemed too good to be true. More stars came out, secretly revealing their heavenly magic to their adopted disciple, who lay in awe on top of the world. Si felt the gentle touch of zero gravity as the weight of the world lifted from the beams beneath his shoulder blades. He searched for the Plough, Ursa Major, Ursa Minor, Polaris, Orion's Belt – but in vain. This sky was brand new, and he was the first to ever witness its majesty.

He was rudely interrupted by a whistle from the

pavement, and quickly descended to rejoin his mates. Darkness had lightened the mood, as it always did. Jase threw a chip at a passing dog, relieving the regret of refusal by stealing a replacement from Jules. Matty trod the tightrope of the kerbstones, passing his chips from hand to hand to redress the imbalance, drawing mocking laughter with relish. Everyone else laughed at Pete's jacket, saying it was a girl's, asking if he borrowed it from his sister, suggesting he could give it to his mum as a birthday present, asking if he had a matching skirt. Jules told a joke about an Englishman, a Scotchman, an Irishman and a Westie, but got it wrong several times and eventually quit while he was behind.

"Anyway, I used to go to Westmoor, you know," said Pete.

"Didn't know it was a girls' school!" Si replied, prompting uproar.

Jase led the way along the estate road, shepherding the flock towards the last brushstrokes of muted light that glazed the hilltops at the edge of the known world. They parted ways at the usual parting of the ways. They all went home and went straight to bed. Except for Si, who delayed the inevitable under the perceived protection of lamppost light.

After spending five minutes trying not to look, he eventually plucked up the courage to survey the route ahead. The sinister alleys, cold lonely yards, and dark forgotten corners of the houses lining the streets in the foreground seemed poorly lit and ill-defined as if the night had fallen from above to blur the edges of the back-door lights and smudge the surfaces of assorted patches of reflecting steel. The semis beyond, however, basked in a golden glow. They seemed somehow unreal, as if painted on black cardboard or carefully placed in parallel positions, like model railway houses. He could see his house, or thought he could, amongst the blurred jumble at the edge of focus range. Everything seemed painfully familiar and dull, like the ornaments on the mantelpiece that nobody liked, that were never cleaned and were constantly ignored but were always there.

Si began to run, aiming initially for the white patch which he thought might be his garage door. Sometimes as he ran, he looked constantly from right to left, checking for movement in the many dark, terrifying spaces along either side of the road, speeding up when each horrifying void approached and quickening again upon passing. Sometimes he ran with his gaze fixed straight ahead, imagining movement in the many dark, terrifying spaces along either side of the road, speeding up when each horrifying void approached and quickening again upon passing. In a final burst of maximum speed, he flashed past the alley that led to the school playing fields, focussing stubbornly on the kitchen light, averting his eyes from the mud-stained, outstretched fingers of the blood-hungry corpses that he'd just woken from their hundred-year sleep under the centre circle. He belatedly slowed to walking pace, having forgotten himself, and looked up in relief to see that no-one was watching. He closed the side door behind him and headed straight for the ever-unreliable reassurance of his second favourite kitchen cupboard.

5

The Perfect Lone Ranger

Si woke, put on clean clothes, straightened the bed, and dumped his dirty clothes in the Ali Baba basket in the bathroom. He washed his hands, face and feet, brushed his teeth, grabbed his tracky top from the bedroom door handle, and headed downstairs for breakfast. Upon entering the kitchen, he noticed an ominous looking envelope partially hidden under a scribbled message. Topped with a clutch of £1 notes, and with everything secured under a dual-purpose knife-cum-paperweight, all had been carefully positioned at his place at the table, where it couldn't be missed. He read the message.

Simon, dad says can you go to pay for the TV and then go to pay for the papers and then get twenty No6s from the bus station shop. He said you can keep the change haha mum x

His heart sank as he knew that it would take until early afternoon. He remembered that Matty and Pete weren't around that day, though, so it wasn't too bad. He decided to go looking for a new school bag while he was there. If there was one he liked, he might be able to get it on Saturday, as there was a Marsdens at the seaside too.

He made some toast and a cup of tea and took up position at his place at the table. He opened the envelope, which contained a paying-in book, and counted the money - £4. He made some more toast. The kitchen window framed a sky of broken clouds, each weighed down by an ominous burden of cement grey, though crowned with diamonds and ribbons of silver and seawater blue. Patchy and uneven, inconclusive and indecipherable, floating flat-bottomed on the invisible, spirit-levelled ceiling of a strata of warm air that towered above the school roof, the ragged army of advancing cumulus gave few clues as to the day ahead.

Deciding he'd probably be OK in his tracky top, he put the empty cup and plate in the sink and checked his favourite kitchen cupboard for new additions (with well-placed pessimism). He stashed the cash inside the paying-in book, slotted the envelope into his inside pocket, pulled the key from the kitchen side of the lock, and exited. He slammed and locked the door, hid the key under the plant pot next to the drain, and headed out into the street.

He decided to walk to town because, as usual, he hadn't been left any money for the bus. The street was eerily quiet and lifeless, the crowded sky seeming ominous and overbearing in stark contrast. A few mums and dads pottered about in gardens and garages, but Si didn't recognise any of them. He liked crowds and didn't mind talking to strangers, but was always anxious and uneasy around anyone unfamiliar on the estate, feeling like they were violating the security and intimacy of his territory.

He scanned the immediate vicinity in the search for reassurance, taking comfort from the sight of one of the older boys from his school perched on a kerbstones farther down the street, sharpening his penknife. His heart sank, though, at this unwelcome reminder of the impending curtailment of his sunlit, boundless, cherished freedom. Images flashed through the empty space just beneath the skin of his forehead: condensation on the bathroom window, pretending to blow smoke on a cold winter's morning, wet kit staining his schoolbooks, the long walk home in the sweltering heat of the first half-term, staring out of the first-floor window of the Atkinson Block, queuing in the rain for last dinners. He knew it wouldn't be as bad as the thought of it, though – like the dentist, or drama lessons, or corn flakes. He crossed the road to avoid any unnecessary, awkward, self-conscious interaction with his schoolmate.

He paid for the papers first as, contrary to the instruction in his mum's note, this made the most sense. Before entering the newsagents, he cautiously took a single pound note from the envelope in his inside pocket. Handing the note over at the counter, his eyes were drawn to the delights of the glass cabinet. On being handed 65p in change, the temptation merely grew, especially as he still had 10p of his own. He decided to be disciplined, though, and to wait until a final reckoning could be made before he spent any more cash, especially as he'd spent a fortune yesterday, about which he now felt regretful and foolish and reckless and naive and exploited and ashamed and remorseful. He put the change with the 10p piece in his back left pocket, making a mental note as the bell tolled deeply, lustily, but unnoticed. £3.75.

Taking the path of least resistance, he followed the bus route to town. He hated walking alone through the no man's land between the shop (which he'd just passed) and the dark, foreboding, sinister stone columns of the railway bridge that marked the gateway to the safety of the town centre. He'd always seen the bridge, not as holding evil within, but as protection from evil without. He hated having time to think, to exaggerate, to amplify, to magnify, to inflate, to embroider. He began to feel the presence of the spirits of the day. He could sense them staring at him along the tarmac of every arterial, from the roof of every end-terrace, through the slits in the drain covers. He could hear them tapping on railings, shaking the branches of trees, and opening and closing hidden doors to forbidden places. He could smell them hiding in the privets, buried under the broken earth of the allotments, concealed in the mounds of cut grass. He tried to think of something else to take his mind off the oppressive, claustrophobic, entirely unfounded threat of danger which he sensed in each and every mundane feature of suburbia, but the harder he tried to take his mind off them, the more the feelings of fear grew. He began to run. Hard and fast. Powerful and graceful. He started to laugh. He was released. Whatever it was back there was left behind, vanquished and exorcised.

Without trying to, he began to think about his route through town. He decided to go to Marsdens first, then the TV shop, then the bus station. That way, when he'd paid for the No6s, he'd know how much he had left to spend on himself and be able to weigh up the relative merits of buying some sweets or taking the bus or both or neither.

Before he had time to allow his fears to resurface, he was approaching the welcoming arms of the railway bridge. Passing under, he gazed up in awe at the weeping, blackened brickwork, the soot-stained, oppressive arches a reminder of the harder, more brutal, less privileged past of his history lessons, which he wished he'd listened to more carefully. He did a slow 360, staring vertically upwards in dizzying, disorientating reverence. Dazzled by a blast of unexpected sunlight, he straightened up to greet the Belisha Beacons, which stood sentry to the town, taking a steadying step to the left as he crossed.

Thirty-nine seconds later, he entered the Riding Arcade through the northern entrance, quickening his step as he passed the men standing outside the bookies. On approaching Marsdens, and hoping not to have to go inside, he breathed a sigh of relief as he saw a selection of branded shoulder bags neatly arranged in the window display. A black bag with a yellow chevron, logo, lettering and trim caught his eye. It was £5, though, and with only £2 hidden in his secret money box at home, he was 50p short of a fifty-fifty split. He reckoned his dad might be in a good mood on Saturday, though, so walked away with guarded optimism.

Sixteen seconds later, he exited the Riding Arcade through the southern entrance, saluting the returning sun to shield his eyes from the dazzling light. The Market Square was unusually busy for a Thursday (the number of shoppers in town on any given day could be predicted fairly accurately, with the accepted ascending order of popularity being Sunday, Tuesday, Thursday, Monday/Friday, Wednesday and Saturday), so his progress across the square was slowed markedly by constantly having to stop to allow people to pass in front of him – being just about old enough to venture into Town unaccompanied, and therefore one of the youngest lone shoppers about, he was clearly at the bottom of the pecking order, and in fact practically invisible.

Finally, he reached the sanctity of the TV shop, which mercifully was on the shady side of the square. The shop was entirely empty of shoppers, so Si walked straight up to the counter, standing in embarrassed self-consciousness for a few seconds before extracting the envelope from his inside pocket and silently handing it over to the TV man. The TV man took the paying-in book out of the envelope, put the three pound notes in the till, wrote an additional payment record in the book, stamped the record in the appropriate column, put the book back into the envelope, and gave the envelope and 5p change back to Si, all without saying a word. Si understood that it was an adult transaction, so he couldn't have a meaningful part to play in the process, either by speaking, or in being spoken to, or in any other way, and preferred it that way.

He left the shop with a sense of relief, release, liberation. The responsibility of responsibility for the notes had weighed heavy in his inside pocket, and he was much more comfortable with the uncomfortable, pendulous jangling of the coins in his left back pocket. A fifty, two tens and two fives. 80p. Retracing his route from two days ago, he headed for the cobbles of the narrow, shaded, claustrophobic approach to the bus station. Climbing the stone steps to the station shop, his path was blocked by the end of the queue. He assumed his place with resigned anxiety, which intensified notably when two boys took up position behind him.

"What you getting?" asked the one who looked a bit older than Si.

"Some No6s for my dad," Si replied.

"Can we buy two separates?" asked the one who looked the same age as Si.

"No. They're for my dad," Si replied.

"What school you go to?" asked the one who looked the same age as Si.

"Manor," Si replied. "You?"

"Westmoor," replied the one who looked a bit older than Si, gesturing with his thumb to indicate that this applied to his mate, too.

Si began to feel very uneasy, as his congeniality amongst strangers didn't extend to anyone under the age of sixteen. He faced forward with forced formality, leaning to his right to analyse the composition and probable speed of the queue, glancing impatiently at his watch like the pensioners in the Post Office. Worryingly, the two boys remained outside the shop, relinquishing their place in the queue. He was safe for now, though the intentions of his new acquaintances began to play on his mind, and he felt the first flutterings of panic. Due to Sod's Law, the queue started shrinking rapidly, and Si was soon at the head.

"Twenty No6s for my dad," requested Si optimistically.

"Which ones?" the shopkeeper replied.

Si pointed to the relevant pack, confident of the colour scheme.

"Fifty-eight," the shopkeeper responded.

Si handed over a fifty and two fives, and received the pack and a two in return. Agreeing to the shopkeeper's request to put them somewhere safe (and knowing that this really meant a number of things, including 'Don't tell anyone you bought them here!', 'They better not be for you!', 'Keep them out of sight!' and 'You better not let me down!'), Si exited in unnecessary haste and with affected urgency. He'd quickly calculated that his dad had in fact allocated 12p for the return bus fare, and decided, in desperation, to sacrifice half of it on the return leg, as this would not only justify seeking the sanctuary of the station concourse but also warrant breaking into a delicately measured half-run-half-walk. If performed with well-practised body shape and the appropriate body language, a half-run-half-walk could guarantee speed but give the impression of unhurried, calm composure.

Avoiding eye contact, he skipped past the two waiting Westies, grateful for the head start that the descending steps gave to his short half-run-half-walk. Knowing that looking back would merely invalidate the credibility of his finely judged movements, he faced directly ahead, his neck frozen in fear. Upon reaching the far side of the road, which he'd crossed with requisite recklessness, and relieved not to hear footsteps following, he slowed down to a quarter-run-three-quarter-walk.

The station mostly consisted of road markings, being merely a wall, a few benches, twelve bus stops and a pointless pedestrian entrance arch, which could be avoided by simply walking around either end of the wall. As soon as he crossed the threshold, he felt the threat of the unknown dissolve, knowing that amongst the discarded tickets, the empty crisp packets, the innumerable fag ends, the abandoned newspapers, the partially crushed pop cans and the utterly ambivalent waiting passengers, his safety was assured.

He sat on the bench between Stand 2 and Stand 3 (he wouldn't normally sit on a bench, but the old lady at the other end offered further protection). To his amazement, the bus appeared moments later. He jumped on with undue haste, risking the wrath of the old lady, who was clearly in front of him in the notional queue, and carefully selected a place on one of the side-facing three-man seats towards the back of the lower deck. He ran the fingers of his left hand over his back left pocket to gauge the size of the three coins, thereby selecting and subsequently extracting one of the two tens. The conductor came to take his fare before the bus departed, as they often did, and Si dropped the change into his back left pocket and proceeded to eat the ticket, which he often did, despite the threat of ejection by the inspector. Six pence wasn't much reward for his efforts, he thought, as the bitter, nauseating taste of the paper filled his jaw and nostrils, though he took some consolation from the fact that he had given the conductor one coin and received two in return, and now had four coins instead of three. He smiled in smug satisfaction. A ten and three twos. 16p.

The bus pulled out of the station through the designated exit gate, turning left to pick up in town. Si spotted the two Westies walking past the camera shop. They were laughing, but he couldn't work out how or why or at what (he knew that laughter was best interpreted as it started or when it finished, and he had missed both ends in this instance). He couldn't tell if they were laughing at something funny or silly, or if they were laughing at him. He couldn't tell if they were laughing with kind hearts or with mean minds. He couldn't tell if they were laughing at something that had just happened or at something they were about to do. He couldn't help wondering, again, if they were laughing at him, and he felt the pain of the possibility across his chest, right on top of the aching of the unknown. He quickly checked ahead to the next stop, but luckily there was no-one waiting, so there was no chance he would be caught up with, overtaken or, worse still, noticed. As the bus passed under the railway bridge, he risked a final sideways glance through the mud-splattered back window, but the view was obscured, blurred, clouded, and the feeling of fear faded into the distance, along with the bank, the jewellers and the estate agents.

Swung to and fro by the unnatural rhythm of the side-on seats, Si soon fell under the spell of their mysterious hypnosis. Staring dead ahead, he strained to hold his eyes in a fixed, motionless gaze as the familiar sights of the suburban roadside flashed by at breakneck speed: railings, hedges, low branches, gateposts, lampposts, telegraph poles.

The bus seemed to slow as it passed the manicured perfection of the cricket field. He scanned from left to right, looking for movements in and around the pavilion, groundsman's shed, clubhouse and scoreboard hut, breaking the spell. The final score from Sunday morning's match was still displayed, and he was struck by a sudden sense of timelessness. He remembered the score creeping slowly up as the heat of the early afternoon took its toll on the outfield. He remembered running to retrieve a ball from beyond the boundary, thrilled with his unappreciated contribution. He remembered a dropped catch, a run-out, a six. He surveyed the scene for signs, but the place seemed abandoned, neglected, forgotten. He imagined the hut in the middle of the night, confirming the score to the bats that swooped above the wicket long after bad light stopped play. He imagined the hut in the middle of winter, the birds on the covers checking the overs played. He imagined the hut in years past and in years to come. He couldn't imagine life without the score displayed, and felt happy and sad.

Leaving the past and future behind, the bus crept slowly uphill towards the parkside stop. Si pressed the overhead bell strip and made his way to the front. The driver stopped reluctantly, as they always did for unaccompanied children, and he jumped off with a single leap, avoiding the unnecessary bottom step.

On landing, he straightened up to study developments in the park. It was unusually quiet, and his friends were nowhere to be seen. He was struck by the crippling fear of missing out, of being overlooked, of his absence not being noticed. He began to run, as he knew he had to drop the paying-in book and No6s at home before returning to the park end, and that it might take ten minutes, a delay which could have calamitous consequences. He was hungry, though, and contemplated making something to eat. Then he checked his watch, acknowledged the significance, and slowed down to a casual, disinterested stroll.

He made slow progress, continually crossing sides just for the hell of it. The estate seemed uncharacteristically content and carefree. Neighbours gossiped over dividing fences, proudly guarding their territory with folded arms. Kids laughed and chased and rode and played and sang and teased and whistled. The coalman slammed a gate as he returned to his truck, wiping his hands on his overalls with a *tra-la-la-la-lee*, the clasp chiming with immaculate timing and in perfect harmony. Si couldn't work out why it seemed different. Maybe it was the light, or the time, or the temperature, or maybe it was him.

Crossing the road for the fifth time, he glanced over his shoulder to check for any traffic approaching from the park end. In the distance, he saw a cart turning onto the estate road, the driver tugging on the reins to steer the horse towards The Birches and The Alders.

He began to run. Terrified of disappointing and desperate to please, he didn't even glance along the alley that led to the school playing fields, sped past his own vacant driveway, and powered up the steps towards Brian's front door. To his delight, he noticed the oily patches dotted along the tarmac where Brian's car was usually parked, realising this would guarantee unqualified approval.

He darted around the side of the house to the back yard, disentangled the pair of discarded bike frames, and balanced one on each of his tightly tensed lower arms.

"Raaagbo! Raaagbo!" came the cry from the street, accompanied by a slow clip-clopping.

Dropping one of the frames near the side door, he carried the heavier of the two recklessly down the steps and out onto the pavement, using his momentum to heave the handlebars up onto the bed of the cart, pushing the back forks onto the wooden slats to ensure secure positioning.

"Hang on, there's another one," Si pleaded.

He rushed back up the steps to collect the lighter frame, panicking unnecessarily as the cart waited motionless. Descending at speed, he almost lost his footing.

"Woa boy!" the driver said, confusing the horse.

Si threw the frame onto the centre of the bed with a single, graceful motion, knowing that the left pedal would be buried safely amongst the assorted fence posts, half-rotten floorboards and electrical cable spaghetti.

"That's your lot," Si confirmed, and the driver instructed the horse to move on with a masterly, mysterious, almost imperceptible flick of the reins.

Si was triply pleased. He'd kept his promise, shown his gratitude for the emergency twos, and made up for unwittingly ignoring his neighbour the previous evening. He tried to stay cool and keep a straight face. However, like every time he scored a goal, he couldn't help but smile. Lifting the plant pot to retrieve the door key, he whistled a cheerful tune.

Searching through his second favourite kitchen cupboard, he found a tin of processed peas and decided to have them in sandwiches. He opened the tin with his camping can opener, which he always used in preference to the butterfly can opener, as it seemed more resourceful, self-reliant and adventurous. He warmed the contents on a low heat, so the juice didn't boil over, and served a carefully approximated third of the peas onto the lower halves of three slices of bread, so as to make fold-over sandwiches. A rare foray into his mum's ingredients cupboard revealed a jar of mint sauce, some of which he poured onto the plate for dipping his sandwiches. After his third processed pea fold-over sandwich, he poured the remaining pea juice onto his plate, stirred in the remnants of the mint sauce, and mopped up every last drop with two more slices of bread, leaving the plate visibly clean.

Twenty-three seconds later, he was back outdoors, the key hidden safely in its usual spot. The street was empty, the air still, the light subdued. He looked in every direction, checking every likely location for signs of activity, but in vain. Undeterred, he closed his eyes and listened for clues, though he couldn't hear a single thing other than the barely audible but relentless high-frequency humming of silence. Opening his eyes, he was reminded of the empty, oppressive lethargy of a school day on the estate, when boredom and listlessness were compounded by chickenpox.

His mood darkening, he decided nevertheless to amble aimlessly in the general direction of the park. He walked in the middle of the street, hoping that an ostentatious, pointless gesture of defiance might lift his sinking spirits, though there was no traffic to make it meaningful. He looked from side to side as if surveying an unfamiliar, potentially menacing neighbourhood for signs of danger, though everything appeared unremarkable, sombre and safe. He saw no attraction in the shapes and shades of the suburban gardens, the colours all rendered less distinguishable by the unwelcome addition of a splash of grey. No sounds cut through from the muted, colourless undertones of the afternoon. There was no sun nor sky, no wind nor clouds, no heat nor cooling breeze. It was a day of nothing.

Avoiding the side entrance, he entered the park through a well-used gap in the fence, expertly contorting his neck, shoulders and back to avoid any loose ends of exposed wire. Struck by an unfamiliar sense of apathy and indecision, he stood motionless and indifferent, wondering where to look first. He headed for the playground, not expecting to find his friends there, but to nevertheless be more visible from every angle, and therefore more likely to be found by them.

He proceeded at a snail's pace, stopping regularly to pull leaves off the bushes. He methodically double-folded each leaf, twice snapping the midrib to create four horizontal sections, which he proceeded to carefully separate and throw over his shoulder as if leaving a trail. The leaves seemed waxy and artificial, like those on the evergreens in the Chinese takeaway. He looked over at the trees lining the park road, their lower branches nodding tired and lifeless, bored of the summer holidays. They looked like the trees in the photos on the cover of the Geography textbook (Book 1): faded and weary, dated and overlooked. Nothing seemed real. Everything seemed like it seems in dreams.

He took up position on the first of the four swings. The remaining swings swung back and forth in barely visible motion, in tribute to their previous occupant and in anticipation of the next. The slide stood lonely and abandoned, discarded crisp packets gathering symbolically at the foot of the steps. The roundabout nestled silently in its casing, resting its bearings. Si looked up to search the clouds for a break, sighing in disappointment at the relentless, oppressive uniformity of the heavens above, a mirror image of the tarmac at his feet. Instead of fractures, he noticed darker, shadowy patches, bottlenecks and jostling for position, discouraging signs. He hung his head, watching the blotches of chewing gum appear and disappear in perpetual, vertical motion between the air holes of his baseball boots.

In the hope of belatedly hooking up with his mates, he conducted a tour of the usual haunts, though he was understandably nervous of asking to join in with whatever they were doing halfway through, as he might spoil the balance or scupper pre-made arrangements or upset the apple cart. He walked along the park road, crossed at the lights, passed the old chapel, and turned thoughtlessly onto School Lane. Despite it being the penultimate weekday of the school holidays, the school car park gates were open, and a yellow Cortina, a blue Cortina, a white Marina and a red Sunny rested immobile in their usual spots. Mindful of the owners, he sprinted beyond view of the classroom windows.

Approaching the Shepherd's lights, he cut off the corner by taking a detour round the back of the pub, vaulting over the low wall into the yard. Careful not to attract the attention of the regulars in the snug, he quietly checked the bins. There were a few mats in one, but he had mints of all of them at home, plus they were all covered in ash, so he left them alone. The other contained several interesting empty bottles for pale ales and cherry brandy, but they were all jammed in tightly, and he knew he'd make a racket if he fished them out, so he left them alone. There were a couple of towels on the line, but lacking encouragement and knowing that he wouldn't benefit from the adulation it deserved, he bottled it. He did the scissors over the wooden fence that separates the pub yard from the pavement, crossed at the crossing, and headed up Heron Hill towards the foot of the quarry steps.

There was no-one to be seen. The sun came out behind the still unbroken clouds, driving its unforgiving anger through the stubborn blanket below. The heat borrowed moisture from above, raining beads of sweat onto Si's forehead and into the space between his shoulder blades. The sky began to brighten, enhancing the eerie, unnatural, premature atmosphere of sterile serenity normally reserved for the first week back at school. He powered purposefully up the steps to The Alders, trying to look like he was returning for a specific reason, in case anyone was looking from the upstairs windows.

He decided to abandon the hunt, realising that to continue meaningfully, he would have to extend his search perimeter, involving a much longer walk with little chance of success and which would, if fruitful, merely make him look desperate. Instead, he headed for the council pitches, where he knew he would find enough to do to kill an hour or two.

He retraced the start of his route from the previous day, this time on foot, turning left off the hospital approach road and taking a shortcut through the grounds of the care home. The care home was one of several officially 'access only' areas that the boys unofficially strolled through with impunity, like the hospital, the mill, the reservoir, the crematorium and the Technical College, even occasionally saving their legs along the corridors, through the lobbies and in and out of the lesser-used doors of the main buildings. He stopped at the touchline of the rugby pitch, giving admirable but pointless respect to the barren and balding playing area. He carefully surveyed the scene, looking particularly for classmates, schoolmates, mates' mates and kids of friends of the family, in that order.

He noticed a group of schoolmates playing cricket on the first of the two football pitches (at least, he recognised most of them as schoolmates, thus rendering the identity of those he didn't recognise as irrelevant). They were mostly older kids, which made the request more awkward, but the reward more satisfying and therefore duly worthy of awe and admiration. It was always easier to ask younger kids, or even to force the issue, but the prize was infinitely more modest and carried the risk of peer detection and days of relentless derision and ridicule. To his delight, he counted eleven players.

By the positioning of the outfield, he could tell that they were using the touchlines, the byline at the hospital end and the centre line as the boundaries. Realising that there were only three fielders (as well as the bowler and wicket-keeper, of course), he saw an opportunity to avoid embarrassment and potential rejection, and ran over to take up position on the vacant touchline, which was luckily also the nearest.

"Come in a bit, to stop singles!" shouted the bowler, to Si's amazement.

He spent the next half-an-hour or so at cover, doing a blameless job in protecting the boundary, stopping everything within his power before throwing to the wicket-keeper with unerring accuracy, and going through the motions with anything beyond reach, rubbing the tennis ball against the pocket of his jeans before returning underarm to the bowler. The bowler and wicket-keeper alternated every over, so he shied away from requesting a turn at bowling, not wanting to threaten a clearly pre-ordained strategy and well-established hierarchy. As the idle players on the batting side sat observing respectfully in two groups of two beyond the centre line boundary, he realised there were still four players to dismiss, assuming the game was observing the usual 'last man standing' rule of junior park cricket.

He took an easy catch, for which he deserved and sought and received no credit. The bowler quickly took a further two catches during a spate of woefully inexperienced batting, leaving a solitary batsman facing the music. To Si's surprise, the bowler moved the fielders deeper. Succumbing to temptation, the batsman fell for it and was immediately run out.

Si took up position on the grass in the off-field half of the rain-starved centre circle, awaiting his teammates with well-disguised terror.

"What's his name?" asked one of his teammates to one of the others, feigning hostility but betraying good humour with the start of a smile.

"Si," one of the others replied.

"He's in the year below," one of the others added.

"Yeah!" Si confirmed in embarrassment. Given the natural pecking order, he had a feeling that he ought to know their names and that they ought not to know his, but he realised that these kinds of things were often not the case, despite popular belief.

Incredibly, he was chosen to bat first, undoubtedly as the result of some tactical calculation on the part of the team leaders, who were becoming apparent.

He survived the first and third overs comfortably, confirming his seriousness and credibility by not scoring a single run. In the fourth over, his partner took a single for the first time, and Si returned to the crease.

Taking a two off the next ball, he was off and running, and reached a creditable fourteen before facing a claim for leg before. In the absence of an umpire, disputes had to be resolved mutually. Being younger, subordinate and a guest, Si felt he had no choice but to agree, and walked. Luckily, his teammates reluctantly concurred, and he was spared ignominy.

He resumed his seat in the centre semi-circle, trying desperately to supress a smile.

"We chose to bowl, and this is the last innings," one of the team leaders confirmed.

"What do we need?" Si asked.

"Sixty-two," one of the team leaders replied.

Si instantly completed a quick calculation: 6 x 14 = 84. Elated at having contributed more than his fair share, he assumed a more relaxed viewing position, resting casually on his left elbow and forearm, and began to chew on grass, as was customary when watching junior park cricket.

Out of the blue, however, he was struck by a sudden sense of anxiety. Why had he been told that his team had chosen to bowl first and that this was the last innings? As he would play no further part in the game, did this mean that his presence was no longer required, and that he was no longer welcome? Had he overstepped the mark by joining his teammates to watch proceedings and caused offence? No! He couldn't be blamed for that, as he didn't know this was the last innings at the time. He did now, though! Should he invent an excuse to leave? No! They might think that was rude. Should he ask if he was allowed to stay? No! They might think he was a bootlicker. Should he try to help with tactics in order to justify his continued attendance? No! They might think he was cocky and arrogant beyond his years.

He was crippled by indecision and, consequently, did nothing other than side with the bowlers and hope for a quick defeat. His prayers were swiftly answered as a sudden batting collapse saw the opposition score a comfortable thirty-run victory. He felt an instant sense of relief and wondered why he had ever cared about what this hopeless set of idiots thought!

Shunning farewells, he crept away unnoticed, hopping over the low hedge into the hospital grounds. He modified his body language upon landing so as to display a purposeful, business-like gait. The lukewarm reception afforded by the cricketers only enhanced his sense of abandonment, and he adopted the contrived, self-pitying air of the outcast.

As always, on these occasions, he was happy to be left alone with big thoughts. He surveyed the western horizon, visible beyond the crest of the emergency access road, low and humble at the border of the featureless fields of the moor, and was over-optimistically convinced that he could detect the curvature of the

Earth. He conjured a relentless procession of vistas as if chasing the distant skyline in never-ending, fruitless pursuit, like the sun. He looked up to see the clouds, finally, begin to semi-detach, giving emphasis to their long journey from the terrifying squall of the ocean, eastwards over the low hills of neighbouring counties, withdrawing in exhaustion towards an early night. He bathed in the heat and light of the sun, the growing holes in the sky allowing its gentle touch to stroke his cheeks and forearms from one hundred million miles away. He was hungry and decided to head for home, and to count the different types of birds on the way to make it quicker.

After identifying several sparrows, five starlings, two magpies (thankfully), two crows and an unexpected pair of seagulls, he arrived back home just in time for tea, which by the magical, miraculous, clairvoyant power of mums, was being laid on the table as he carelessly kicked off his baseball boots. Following a tea of minced beef, mash and peas (it was Thursday, after all), he escaped upstairs into his room, hoping to avoid the usual family inquisition into the events of his day.

He was feeling sorry for himself and decided to stay in for the evening. He didn't want to endure the embarrassment of explaining his absence during the day, and knew it would be easier to brush off in the morning.

He decided to look through, sort out and tidy up his drawers, and to throw away anything superfluous that had accumulated since he last did it on his birthday. Not wanting to constantly have to get up and down, he put his favourite radio compilation tape on 'play both sides/ repeat' first. He inspected his fossil boxes, replacing the decaying packing tissue with toilet paper stolen from the bathroom before separating the ammonites from the plants and stacking them neatly in opposite corners at the back of his bottom drawer. Next, he carefully collected all the old pennies strewn randomly amongst the partially obscured ephemera of the lower layer, before separating the Victorias from the two Edwards and the two Georges and storing them in three newly emptied tobacco tins, the contents of which had been sacrificed for the purpose. With great satisfaction, he discovered the tins fitted snugly in a single, roughly chronological row across the middle of the base: first, second/fourth, third/fifth. Then he sorted out his medals, belt buckles and paper/card collectibles, which largely involved getting them out, looking at them with disinterest, and putting them back neatly. Upon completion, he took great pride from the rationality of the new arrangement: front – mostly Second World War; middle – mostly pre-war; back – one hundred million years plus.

Turning his attention to the middle and top drawers, he felt his enthusiasm begin to wane, and he resorted to a quick, perfunctory rearrangement, sorting his cig vouchers into fives and twos and sticking his loose stamps into his Stamp Saver Book. The tens took him over halfway, but the seemingly endless strips of singles barely proved their worth, completing less than two additional pages and leaving a sickly, nauseating taste in the mouth. A quick pruning of the worthless, pointless and frivolous, and he was done.

He lay in bed, staring at the ceiling. He listened as Side One, Track Two stumbled clumsily into Side One, Track Three for a second time, and cursed his poor stop/start editing. He traced the lines in the overhead plaster onto non-existent paper, closing one eye to sharpen the focus of his fingernail. He searched for wisps of cobwebs around the coving, deciding to sweep them away with his golf glove and seven iron whenever he could be bothered. He checked his posters for bleaching, loose corners and misalignment, though all seemed in order. He inspected the tops of his drawers, dressing table and wardrobe for misplacement, though everything occupied its carefully considered, correct position.

He cursed himself for wasting the day. He tried to imagine what his friends might have said about him on first noticing his absence, or whenever they needed his help with the usual kinds of things (speaking to adults, bike maintenance, the Highway Code, directions), or, worse still, when reminiscing. He decided he'd probably got off relatively light, with perhaps just the usual gentle mockery of his quietness, seriousness and pointless conscientiousness at school. He certainly wouldn't have attracted the withering criticism very occasionally directed at Jules and Jay, and was in fact most likely, along with Pete and Matty, amongst the few who were universally admired within the group.

He thought of all the things he could have done with the day. He could have bought a day ticket and had an adventure on the buses and trains. He would have travelled to one of the boundary stations and had his packed lunch on the hills between transport zones. He could have gone on a solo bike ride. He wouldn't have been hindered by constant pit stops, disagreements over directions, and the consequent disappointing compromises. He could have gone hunting for bits and pieces. He would have sought the shelter of the trees in the woods, the forest and the plantation, keeping his head down to avoid detection, and would have kept his discoveries in neat little piles in the undergrowth to return to later (like a wolf returning to its prey, he liked to think). Or he could have just taken a blanket and had a shoe box picnic in a secluded spot on the reclaimed slopes of the quarry. He would have hidden in the long grass to watch the late afternoon sun explode in heavenly patches across the otherwise monochrome moor, its brilliant rays smashing holes in the submissive sky, the dazzling light darting to the grateful Earth in celestial shafts before crawling sluggishly over the fields and hedgerows in search of lost souls below. Tortured by regret, he fell asleep.

6

A Flash of Time

Shaun stirred in his bed, fighting a losing battle against the inevitable victory of the day. He was paying a painful penance in the semi-conscious purgatory between the unsuspecting joy of sleep and the private hell of the commute, timecard and warehouse. He woke to a dry mouth, heavy eyes and a familiar sense of light-headedness, brought on as usual by a temporary loss of memory. He took a drink of water from the pint glass that he'd sensibly but uncharacteristically placed, for emergencies, on his bedside table. It went down easily, and he knew that he would soon start to feel better, as he usually did after the gentle introduction of a Thursday evening.

He put on his work clothes, combed his hair, and disabled the rarely needed alarm on his bedside clock, thereby passing the point of no return. He headed for the bathroom, laughing out loud as he passed Si's half-open bedroom door. His brother was curled up on top of the blankets with his playing-out clothes still on. He washed, scrubbing the ends of the index and middle finger of his right hand with the nailbrush. He brushed his teeth, combed his hair a second time, and headed downstairs.

His mum had a cup of tea, four slices of toast, his freshly prepared lunch box and a flask of coffee ready and waiting on the kitchen table.

"Friday, at last!" he exclaimed, as joyfully as his customary lack of enthusiasm allowed.

"Come straight home from work tonight, won't you? Let's not have a repeat of last week's performance!" his mum pleaded.

"Yeah, OK," he agreed, concealing a knowing smile. It was 7.49.

By 7.57 he was stood at the bus stop. There were a couple of buses just after the hour. The earlier one dropped off slightly further from work, but he usually took it anyway, just to be on the safe side. To his delight, the later bus turned up first, four minutes early. This happened a couple of times every month and always brightened his mood, especially on a Friday, when the dispiriting, doleful, demoralising predictability of routine was marginally more bearable.

As usual, the bus was almost full. Self-consciously, he searched for a place to sit, reaching the penultimate row of the top deck before he found an empty double seat, mercifully vacated seconds earlier by someone getting off at the next stop. Another lucky omen! He flipped the tape in his portable, put his headphones on, and settled down for the long journey. It was 8.04.

As it was the week's end, he decided to plan his budget for the next seven days. He would draw £52.52, though he rounded it down to £50 to simplify the calculations and to give himself an emergency reserve. His board was £10, transport up to £2, catalogue fixed at £4, bookies up to £5 and subs fixed at £3. That would leave at least £10 for both Friday and Saturday nights and at least £6 for Sunday night, unless he got lucky on the horses. This way, he'd probably have something left over for the unexpected during next week, though Thursday night might very reluctantly be sacrificed, as it occasionally was if it had to be. The money made it all worth it. Plus, he only had seven hours to get through today, as it was a half four finish on Fridays.

He concentrated on the music, using his time wisely by memorising the handwritten track listings on the sleeve, in case he needed to know the correct order at any time over the weekend (it was a C90s, and had an album on each side, as available space normally allowed). The songs meant everything to him, setting him apart from the other passengers on the bus, holding him aloft above the pedestrians on the pavement below, pulling him ever further apart from his workmates, neighbours, strangers, leaving a yawning gulf between. He shared them with a select group, amongst whom they cemented an unspoken bond, tempered by joint devotion. They were the inanimate, supernatural ties connecting the fanatical disciples of a wider family too, a family of which he was a proud, anonymous member.

He marked off each milestone along the route in a vain attempt to conjure an illusion of speed. The car showroom, the library, the old synagogue, the Tech, The Swan, the zebra crossing, the substation, the Lion lights. Each tired sight slipped by with dismal, uninviting familiarity, breeding contempt. He was exhausted with riding these same streets, weary of waiting to pull out onto Church Road, drained by the endless detours into nameless estates, worn out with the anguished, fitful struggle up Chapel Hill. He was desperate for a way out, though short-term, it was out of the question (he decided to amend his weekly budget to allow for a £5 allocation for savings). For the time being, he would escape further into his inner circle instead: digging deeper, lingering longer, pushing harder and with more intensity.

It was 8.38. Not far to go now. He balked at the sickening stench of the top deck, sneering at the mindless acquiescence of the habitual smokers. As soon as he was able to do so without attracting unwarranted attention, he rang the bell and descended to the marginally fresher air below. He got off the bus at 8.42, walked the short distance to work, and clocked on at quarter to nine. He bought a coffee from the vending machine (5p) and took a seat at an isolated, empty table in the canteen at 8.47. Avoiding eye contact, pointless small talk and, most of all, any unwelcome premature instructions, he savoured his drink in the unexpected luxury of at least thirteen stolen minutes.

Not wanting to push his luck any further, at 9.02 he ventured out onto the shop floor. 9.04. Told to report to the loading bay to help unload a delivery of clothing. He read the delivery note. Six lines: three of four colours, one of five designs, two of six colours. Twenty-nine separate pallets. First, he helped to load the boxes onto the belt. Then he helped lay out the pallets and stack the boxes accordingly: side-on, five to a row, three horizontally, two vertically, offset. Then he took the lead in dragging the pallets to their allocated places under the pick shelves.

Five to ten. Told to report to the supervisor's office. Given a pick sheet, mostly household textiles (towels, bedding, curtains, etc.), five locations, minimum of five lines each. He decided to use a trolley. Partially assembling five new cardboard boxes by securing the bases with his tape gun, he set off along the one-way system. Simultaneously picking for each of the five locations, he double-checked the sheet at the start of each row to avoid having to retrace his steps.

10.32. Finished first pick.

10.35. Returned to office. Given another pick sheet. Accessories: socks, ties, belts, cufflinks, hankies, etc. Triple shelving, little fiddly boxes, tiny labels. Nightmare!

At eleven, he abandoned his trolley mid-aisle to return to the canteen for a tea break. Steering clear of conversation, he picked up one of the newspapers that were invariably left lying around for general usage and pretended to be interested in the football coverage (being a Friday, there were no results or match reports).

At 11.12, he returned to his trolley. 12.22. Second pick finally finished. 12.25. Returned to office. Told to go across to Hung Garments. He read the despatch notes. Luckily, everything was ready and waiting at the bottom end of the pick area, and he just had to transfer the hangers onto the corresponding rails. Easy job. He told the supervisor that he'd finish it off before he went for lunch. He knew that, with everyone else in the canteen, he'd be able to take it steady. Plus, he'd be able to eat his lunch alone. Plus, he wouldn't have to work to the bell, so he'd probably be able to steal an extra five minutes or more, and they would still think it was him that was doing them a favour! Win times four.

13.22. Completed task in Hung Garments. 13.34. Having noticed the return of the Hung Garments Supervisor, pretended to just finish off and announced his departure for lunch.

13.36. Ate lunch and drank all the coffee in his flask. 13.45. Aimlessly turned cards from the top of the pack, checked out the listings in the paper, scribbled on the back of the paper with the scorer's pen, emptied the ashtrays into the bin, stared blankly at the leak-stained ceiling tiles. 14.09. Counted the time left. Two hours, twenty-one minutes. Returned to office.

14.11. Given another pick sheet, all menswear. Three locations, twenty plus lines each. Piece of cake! Three open boxes on the trolley, thrown all in at leisure, strolled round at a snail's pace, minimum effort for maximum return!

15.20. Third pick finished, returned to office. 15.22. Told that the warehouse was closing for the weekend, that there wouldn't be any overtime, so he needed to walk round tidying up the aisles, ready for Monday.

Immediately recognising this as a sign that all the meaningful work had been completed for the week, he put on an oft-used, well-rehearsed virtuoso performance: appearing singularly busy when all around seemed underemployed, whilst in fact doing absolutely nothing of any real value.

15.28. Strolled purposefully up and down the aisles, avoiding detection with a visible show of resolution and intent. 15.39. Looked at the labels on the pick shelf boxes, sometimes pointlessly rearranging the contents with a feigned sense of willing. 15.49. Stared up at the restock shelves with affected intention, not looking for something that he didn't want to find. 15.55. Nipped to the toilet, not wanting to waste his single permitted afternoon visit. 16.02. Read the handwritten labels on the palletised boxes in despatch, looking for non-existent, incorrectly allocated orders (needle in a haystack). 16.09. Needlessly checked that the number of boxes on each of the pallets bound for Wales reconciled with the number indicated on each on the despatch notes for each location. 16.22. Repositioned a few boxes on a few pallets so as to reduce the risk of a fall. 16.25. Collected his lunch box and flask. 16.26. Hung around in the canteen, not wanting to be first in the queue. 16.27. Collected his wage packet from the servery and counted the contents. 16.28. Took up an anonymous, non-partisan, uncontroversial central position in the queue. 16.29. 16.29. 16.29. 16.30. 16.30 and thirty seconds. He punched the clock.

Released into the pale light of the late afternoon, everything looked different. He decided to walk to town and maybe get a bus from there, or maybe walk. Town looked bigger, busier, brighter, less uninviting.

The early finish gave Shaun time to get things going, to ease himself in, to get a head start. He had sixty-four and a half hours, so if he made the most of the first 150 minutes, he would have achieved something, filled a vacant space, set the right tone, and all before the recognised start-time. That way, he could set off at seven, have a satisfying sixty-two hours left, but already have a tale to tell.

He spent the first half an hour window shopping, counting the minutes until opening time. Tiring of his reflection, of the fading allure of the racks and shelves, of the broken promise of the new, he decided to head for the bookies.

The place was thick with smoke, though only a handful of punters perused tomorrow's runners, facing the wall like naughty children. The board marker displayed the tell-tale signs of a busy afternoon, his shirt stained with ash, his bin overflowing, his knuckles discoloured with non-permanent ink. Shaun glanced at the results board, noticing that a solitary race had yet to be run. He checked the handwritten odds on the last remaining racecard for amendments, the board man poised to pounce as the runners and riders went down. One horse was coming in, from sevens to fives, third favourite, just how he liked them! He filled in a slip. Forgotten Sunset. 5/1. 50p win (he left the tax section blank. There were two schools of thought, bitterly divided over the wisdom of paying tax either on your stake or on your potential winnings, but he had been won over by the absolute certainty that the bookies always take more from you than you take from them).

The start of the race was announced, though it was a mile and twoer, so the cashier quickly took the price and put the bet through anyway. The last few stragglers crowded round the speaker to listen to the early stages. The commentator's voice was rich, distant, dispassionate, and Shaun lost interest. He scoured the floor for lost cash, though the carpet was barely visible in places under the sea of pencils, cig ends and pink slips. Losers. He was struck by an unfamiliar sense of ambivalence. He loved the bookies! He marvelled at the board marker's columns, rows and impeccable handwriting. He relished studying the form, jockeys, owners, trainers, horses for courses. He calculated the odds, counted his winnings, cut his losses, understood the permutations. But. He noticed a pocket-soiled newspaper, the racing pages embellished in obliging blue biro, the text muddied and worn in resignation, the corners bent and broken with submissive old age. It had been abandoned, no longer of practical use. He looked over as the last remaining worshippers beseeched the sacred airwaves, begging for mercy. Their prayers unanswered, they scattered like sinners. Second place. Not bad for a third favourite. Encouraging. He went to the gents to justify his continued presence, then left. It was 17.24 and getting close.

Shunning the indignity of doorstepping, at 17.35, he eventually sought sanctuary. Deciding to prioritise value for money, he called in at The Lion. The place was almost empty, the ever-punctual coven of territorial, hostile, outraged regulars slumped possessively on their allotted stools at the bar providing the only signs of half-life. He ran the gauntlet with his customary dismissive, contemptuous air of superiority and ordered a drink.

Settling in a quiet corner of the lounge, he took his first sip. The place looked weary and dog-eared, though the frosted windows, horse brasses and polished copperware made a vague suggestion of self-indulgence. The bottles behind the bar were neglected and unloved, their time-worn labels showing the stains of former glories, bygone splendour, fading memories. Blotched and blackened by years of indifference and intemperate mistreatment, the upholstery had begun to fray and unravel under the constant strain of work jeans and overalls. Bruised and battle-scarred, the beer-stained carpet lay prone and defeated, the memory of its mesmeric pattern momentarily evoked by the lights of the bandits. It was the perfect place to start, so he bought another drink.

Eventually tiring of The Lion, he made a sharp, unannounced exit through the side door and crossed the road to The Bull, entering through the main door. The bar itself was unoccupied, though a quick, informal glance around the main room confirmed that the tables were thronged with all-dayers and early starters, as he had suspected. He bought a drink and took up a neutral but visible place at the end of the bar. He took a first good look around and was thankful to notice that he half-recognised some of the faces in the crowd, guaranteeing the propriety of his presence. Satisfied with the suitability of his place, position and timing, he began to relax, took a long drink, and lit a cig.

He started to feel the effects, the stresses and strains of the day slowly drifting away with the cig smoke. Two lads were stood at the jukebox, debating passionately. He half-knew who they were, and half-knew who they hung around with, and was confident of a positive result.

His end of the bar faced the front window. He watched as the rivers of the world flowed by along opposing, linear courses, passing obliviously through the clear space between the etched, floral borders of the ancient glass, elevating the detached, composed perspective of his slowly emerging good mood. The bar was lit from above, the slumped shoulders of half-empty bottles and broken ribs of decorative decanters glistening with mystical, hypnotising charm, like the light of the sun on deep, dangerous waters. The music, the smoke, the voices, the drink, the lights, the glass, the wood, laughter, footsteps, dark corners, dazzling reflections. He was under their spell, a willing victim of strange magic.

"Hey! Come over!" a voice called from behind.

It was one of the lads from the jukebox, both of whom nodded towards an empty stool in their quiet corner. Shaun knew that, if his suspicions as to their identities were confirmed, the acute awareness and deep reverence of their shared tastes and interests would be mutual, and he duly took a seat at the table. They were who he thought they were, so they talked about music. Shaun laughed and enthused and listened and explained and acknowledged and agreed and remembered. He gave opinions and disagreed with others with uncharacteristic fervour. He tasted the exhilaration of newly formed, distant friendship, smoking and drinking with renewed ardour, his behaviour and body language betraying a heightened, animated mood. As a moment's hush unexpectedly fell into their corner, all three blew a satisfied, celebratory stream of smoke upwards into the air, their heads tilted back in a dramatic, defiant gesture of victory.

The two lads departed with a muted, unconvincing promise to reconvene at an unspecified future date. Shaun stayed in the quiet corner, brimming with renewed confidence and bristling with an electrifying sense of excitement. He'd made a great start! The place started to empty, though, so he decided to move on.

He burst out through the front door into the unsuspecting street. Cars and lorries and kids on bikes and bus stop birds flew past unnoticed and not noticing. He felt protected by an invisible force, shielded from harm by the captivating combination of alcohol, nicotine, good humour, optimism and the mercifully slow ticking of the weekend clock. He wandered aimlessly, cheerfully, absentmindedly, concluding eventually that it was time to head home. Deciding to get the bus after all, he headed for the station.

He climbed the stairs and claimed the sole remaining empty double seat on the shady side. Soon after departure, however, as the bus emerged from the shadowy sanctuary of the railway bridge, he realised that he'd made a schoolboy error and would have to suffer the sun for most of the rest of the journey. He hid his face from the light, burying his eyes in the ink-stained folds of his sweatshirt sleeve, resting his forehead on the cool, comforting chrome of the seat in front. The bus rocked gently, metronomically, incessantly. Feeling the weight of the week hanging heavily between his temples, he drifted gratefully off to rewarding, profitable sleep.

He woke with a jolt. Straining to focus beyond the unwelcome attentions of the descent of the day, he eventually traced the outlines of the off-licence, post office and bakery. As always, he had woken at precisely the right moment (every morning, he rose within five minutes of his alarm going off and never had to suffer it). He jumped off the bus and vaulted the park wall, mindful that time was of the essence.

Upon returning home, he promptly got down to business: eating his tea, paying his board, adding his share of the scheduled catalogue payment to the clutch of notes in the flour jar, ironing his shirt, stealing an envelope from his dad's rarely used stationery set in which to hide his latest savings fund, wiping down his shoes (he intended heading home earlyish tonight, and might not need the shoes, but he knew how it often went). He took a little longer in the bath, as he had allowed time for it. He lay with his head under the hot water, holding his nose, wallowing in the splendid isolation of unseeing eyes, deaf ears, contented skin. He felt the weight of the week lifting, melting, evaporating, dissolving in the fluid of his joints, thawing in the marrow of his bones, condensing on the mirror. He let the water cool before getting out.

He dried off, brushed his teeth, threw his work gear into the washing basket, ran naked across the landing, and quickly put on clean clothes. Thankfully, his mum had hung the newly ironed shirt in his bedroom, saving him an embarrassing trip downstairs. He combed his hair, drew two satisfyingly crisp £10 notes from his wage packet, dropped his loose change into the now more than half-empty wage packet (to compensate for the potential overspend) and put the remaining cigs from three almost empty packs into a single, consequently almost full pack. He grabbed his jacket from the wardrobe, skipped excitedly downstairs, bid his farewells, collected his single spare key from the ashtray in the kitchen (no point in carrying and risking the bunch) and headed out into the night.

18.45. He had decided to wear his burgundy double-layer jacket with the zipped pockets. Though equally intense at the death of afternoon, the heat of the day had begun to slowly dissipate after teatime recently, leaving a cooling sense of regret and missed opportunity hanging in the air. Each soft, whispered breath of wind carried the veiled threat of autumn.

He took the shortest route to Viaduct Street, trespassing the hospital grounds, skirting the allotments, nipping down cobbled ginnels, cutting through cut-throughs, reluctantly walking the occasional short stretch of connecting pavement between much-loved short cuts. As he was the unofficial coordinator, he stopped off at a phone box to make three confirmation-only calls, keeping it brief each time to avoid spending more than 6p. All sorted.

Arriving at The Feathers ten minutes early, he bought a drink, rested it carefully on a mat in the centre of the table at their usual place at the back of the lounge near the window (to mark their customarily recognised territory). He lit a cig and took up position in front of the bandit, feeding it coins to avoid anxiety, discomfort and the potential embarrassment of sitting alone at the table (as opposed to sitting alone at the bar, which was entirely risk-free). He didn't really know what he was doing, though, as he rarely played the slots and was unfamiliar with the recognised strategies, universal tricks and well-known tell-tale signs. He always said the slots were a mug's game: percentage pay-outs, no skill or judgement required, guaranteed long-term losses. He hoped he hadn't drunkenly shared this with prying eyes. He hadn't been observing the latest developments either, was in the dark as to the recent ins and outs, oblivious as to the chances. He began to feel the curse of creeping self-consciousness, the strain of being observed from behind, the dread of unseen, mocking disapproval. Noticing a pile of local listings on the shelf to one side, he saw a quick way out. He cut his losses and took up position at the table, safely hidden behind a full glass, filling the vacuum by slowly overlooking the dismissed text and disregarded photos, and by quickly emptying the glass.

Two of his mates, Danny and the other Shaun, entered together, saving the day. The last of the quartet, Daz, arrived just in time to be included in the round, keeping it simple. They spent the next ninety minutes or so sharing the usual updates and providing fresh insights: annoying supervisors, awkward jobs, born grafters, useless no-hopers, new procedures, regular customers, latest products, typical responses. The room was full now, the table cluttered, the lights lowered, the air thick with smoke, the ashtray overflowing, the silence shattered. A brighter, clearer, cleaner, less claustrophobic aura illuminated the room, its gentle glow reflected off the top of the tables, captured in the rim of every glass, fractured by the facets of the ashtrays, mirrored by the windows, lighting up eyes.

It was time to move on. Danny and Daz led the way, neither seeking instruction, direction nor consultation. Shaun felt good to be on the move again. He was going places, breaking chains, leaving it all behind. He walked with uncharacteristic swagger: gesturing with his hands, disapproving with his eyes, nodding in agreement, shrugging his shoulders, stopping for effect. It was a rare moment of fulfilment with no regrets, nothing missing, everything in place, nowhere better. The sun had gone, the darkness of the day giving way to the brilliant, dazzling light of night.

Avoiding the main entrance, they slipped unnoticed across the car park, through the fire door, and into the back room of The Ship. The place was heaving. Luckily, they found an empty table on the mezzanine floor, away from the menacing, posturing horde at the bar. Cursing the luck of the draw, the other Shaun went to get the drinks, confident with carrying four. He returned to an empty table, the other three having secured a safer, more secluded spot against the back wall, further from the bar. All the drinks were the same, so the waiting trio each carefully selected a random drink, suitably impressed.

The music blared, putting paid to small talk, though the mob at the bar maintained an incessant, ostentatious big talk. Shaun felt good, though, despite the ill-fitting atmosphere and his ill-suited perspective. It was a passing-through place, a place to show your face, a place to stand tall, to stake a claim, to maintain a presence, to keep in reserve for dark nights, rainy days, emergencies. He surveyed the room with uninhibited pride, with distain and delight in equal measure. What a great song! A strange sensation swelled behind his eyes, between his cheekbones, in his jaw. It was contentment, eminence, honour. He lit a cig before taking his first sip, as that was the natural order of the world.

Just the one later, they left via the main entrance, thanking the bemused doorman as they skipped down the steps.

"I hate that place," the other Shaun admitted, prompting a knowing, recognising, agreeing, acknowledging bout of shared laughter.

Crossing the road to The Duke, they returned to safe territory. It was two-deep at the bar, so three of them stayed outside while Daz went in for the first round of the second sequence. They took up position on the low roadside wall, facing the bay window, cheering as Daz returned triumphant, juggling four glasses. Shaun was glad that he often drank bottles, as he could shove one in his pocket when it was his round and thereby dodge the challenge without losing face.

"Did you hear about Chuck?" asked Daz. "Got caught up in a raid at The Lion last Saturday. He went in through the back just as they were going in through the front. When he turned round to go back out, two of them appeared at the back door. They let him go though, cos he hadn't bought a drink. Said he was looking for his dad."

"They must have been doing the rounds," Danny added. "Lad at work was out in a beer garden somewhere over his way same day. It's got a big fence and you can't see in from the street, so they all thought they were safe as houses. Four of them walked straight through the pub without even checking inside. They were all trapped and no escape. Police just gave them all a telling off though. Probably couldn't be bothered with all the paperwork."

"I know a lad," the other Shaun said. "His dad sent him to the shop to buy some cans. On the way back he got stopped by a patrol car. Told them that he'd asked a bloke to go into the shop for him, cos he didn't want to get the shopkeeper into trouble. They took him back home and told his dad what he'd said. His dad just tut-tutted with a big smile on his face. Shopkeeper and dad both got off scot-free. He got a telling off. Had to go to the station next day and everything!"

They all laughed.

"Reminds me of when we got back from the school camping trip," said Danny. "Me and Shaun and a few others were play-fighting in the church car park on the way home, and I was getting a pasting. Mr Firth saw us out of his office window. He shouted us all back. Said we were all being disrespectful. We all still had our walking boots on, so he asked if anyone had their school pumps in their bag. Thing is, Daz had nicked two rugby balls from the storeroom at the back of the hut on the last day of the trip. He said he didn't have room for both in his bag, so he made me put one in mine. I could tell that Firthy was about to check the bags, so I pulled my pumps out sharpish, cos I was first in line. He gave us all a couple with a pump. Outside, I got more of the same, except you couldn't really call it play-fighting this time cos I got it twice as bad for being a little creep and giving Firthy the pumps. Thing is, the coach driver had already dropped Daz off at the lights on the way back up to school, so he was already home and dry. I called in to drop the ball off on the way home, so Daz ended up with two balls and I ended up with two red ones on the cheeks and a dozen bruises. Daz didn't find it in the slightest bit funny!"

"I was nearly sick!" laughed Daz.

They all laughed.

"We should go there again," Shaun suggested. "Forget the hut! We should get a B&B in town. We could do a crawl around all the pubs around the harbour and get a boat and sail round to where that guy pulled up onto the beach with the dogs or we could just get some take-outs and sit on those rocks near the pier. We could go on the coach. I'll get the tickets this time!"

They all laughed, at the other Shaun's expense.

"The hut's not there anymore," said someone who they barely knew. "It fell apart!"

They all laughed, as did more people who they barely knew.

"Let's all go anyway!" Shaun shouted, though he instantly regretted it, as he was lost for any more words. He took a long drink to dilute the burning blood that had rushed with unseemly haste to the empty space on both sides of his face. Hoping to get as far away as possible from the centre of attention, he decided to concentrate quietly on his idea for a while. He liked to plan ahead, to have something to look forward to, to write things up on the calendar. He liked to think about the old days too, though. After all, he was nearly seventeen now, and getting old.

The night was alive with song, speech, laughter, exaggeration, contradiction, confirmation, compliance. The groups outside were fluid, flexible, versatile, each with its own moving, detachable parts flitting from party to party with a bold, vital energy like fireflies. Moments flashed past unnoticed. Minutes slipped by in seconds. Hours passed imperceptibly, like satellites across the star-studded sky, seemingly slow but gone in a flash of time.

Shaun had lost full control, and the other three had disappeared. He decided to sit inside. His night was starting to dissolve and dissipate, losing form and structure, like the last orders ice at the bottom of the bucket. He fixated on the lights of the bar as they teetered on the edge of focus, their spellbinding witchcraft beckoning an endless stream of willing victims into the lair, the captivating colours reflected in time-worn mirrors, the gems and diamonds glistening in greedy eyes. He leant back, resting his shoulder blades against the wooden frame of the upholstered benching, and smiled. He felt detached, victorious, oblivious. The sound and motion of the room seemed to smudge, soften, coalesce, intermingling in a storm of confusion from which he was sheltered, safe in his cocoon of tables, chairs, beer mats and ashtrays. He lit a triumphant, celebratory cig.

He was exhausted, so he decided to head home. He walked in short spurts, stopping off at the usual places to draw breath and recompose: the wall beside the petrol station, the bench on Church Lane, the pews in the lychgate at St Mary's. Using street furniture, he created a series of quarter milestones (zebra crossing, traffic island, phone box, phone box, phone box), hoping to ease the strain of each clumsy, painful step, walking a middle line between alternating, offset paving stones. He looked up at the sky, using the stars to refocus, readjust, take stock. He sneered in disgust at the kerbstones and gutter, laughed in contempt at the gates and fences, grinned in derision at each passing lamppost, despaired of the potholes and double yellows. The shell of the spell had broken, crushed under his faltering heels, doubt, regret and unanswered yearning seeping slowly into the cracks in the pitiless pavement.

Finally, he arrived safely home. He checked his pockets and was delighted when the second and third cash count reconciled at £11.42. He had made sacrifices, having walked every leg of the night's journey, but he was back now, job done! Plus, it hadn't been too bad. Plus, he could have a lie-in tomorrow. Plus, having shunned a taxi, he'd have at least eleven pound-odd for the day, rather than just eight pound-odd, and that made a world of difference. He looked in the fridge.

Fearful of a repeat of the boil-in-the-bag incident, his mum had prepared some cheese sandwiches (just in case he wanted them) which she had carefully packed in the trusty Tupperware box (so they could be eaten later, just in case he didn't want them).

He took the sandwiches up to his bedroom and polished them off at record speed, washing them down with a pint of milk straight from the bottle. He'd pay for that! Rescuing his portable from beneath the mountain of junk on his dressing table, he flipped the tape, put the headphones on, and lay back in bed. The music was from another time, another place, a distinct moment, though the spectre in the song cast its dark shadow effortlessly through time and space, haunting the present with its unworldly power.

He turned off the bedside lamp, though the electric blue digits of his alarm clock cast eerie shadows onto the folds of his top blanket. 11.49. He could hear much better in the semi-darkness. The song seemed to fill the room. Its raw energy bristled in each dark corner, its uncut force reverberating against the walls and ceiling, the crude intensity creaking in the floorboards. With the volume on full, he was forced to resort to adjusting the headphones. He tightened the headband, palms pressed against cheekbones to wring out every last drop.

The music evoked echoes and images of the city: the towering consequence of the grand hotels and embassies, the welcome reassurance of the backstreet lights, the brutal truth of the doorways and pavements, the shrill call of braking taxis. He was struck by a familiar, desperate longing, tinged for once with a resolute, unwavering shade of optimism. He had made a great start. Still short of seven and a half hours. Over fifty-seven left. In front financially. A little bit left over to put aside.

Plenty of time to put a plan together over the weekend. Make it formal. Convince everyone to commit. Then they'd have to put a plan in place, or face letting the side down. Maybe he would make a few calls to see if he could find a place to stay. Maybe he would get everyone to pay up front for the train, then they'd be halfway there. Maybe he would ask for some cash for his seventeenth.

Satisfied with the opening stages, and with no need to prolong the day, he succumbed to the inevitable. 11.54. Fifty-seven plus!

7

Us or the World

Shaun woke at 7.12, again at 8.42, again at 9.26 and finally at 9.55, eventually forcing himself to get up before the last two digits arrived at the threshold of another hour. His head was still heavy with the weight of the week, his eyes straining under the burden of daylight, his nose congested from the constant stream of stale air, his mouth dry from the relentless intake of fluid. He sat on the edge of his bed, head in hands. He could feel the blood pumping at his temples, his laboured breath straining to circulate through smoke-stained lungs, the poison coursing through his stomach. He put on his dressing-gown and headed downstairs.

All was quiet in the living room and kitchen, and he suddenly remembered that all the others had gone on the trip. He laughed out loud in relief and delight, knowing that the solitude would ease the pain of the tortuous, empty, wasted hours of Saturday morning. Not daring to risk eating, he made a cup of black coffee and took a half-empty bottle of milk from the top shelf of the fridge, realising he had drunk a full pint last night, and that the half-empty bottle would have been delivered in the morning. The two full bottles of red-top that stood unexpectedly on the bottom shelf must have been shop-bought by Si shortly before departure at nine a.m. He transferred 40p from his key tray on the sideboard into the milk jug on top of the fridge, according to the accepted, pre-agreed protocol.

Resting his drinks on the tiles of the hearth, he switched on the TV and took pride of place in his dad's chair, stealing a couple of painkillers from the bottle on the mantlepiece and washing them down with milk before adopting his customary recovery position. He straightened his back, tilted his face up towards the ceiling, closed his eyes, and took a series of deep, penetrating breaths. He felt the fluid in his brain resettling, percolating slowly through a fog of half-formed images, broken bits of memories, muffled voices, eventually seeking solace in the swelling pool of cool, clear, tranquil water that was gradually coalescing in the space between his ears. He felt the interplay of the bones in his neck, analysed the wallpaper on opposing walls to exercise the joints, heard the listless tissue at the nape surrendering like fresh snow crushed under monkey boots. He felt a chasm expand in the empty space between his lungs and stomach, forcing rancid air into the hole at the bottom of his throat, threatening the well-rehearsed efficacy of the healing process. He kept breathing long, hard, steady. And again. And again. Eventually, he felt the gentle touch of forgiveness, the soft caress of mercy, the kindness of time. The load began to lighten. Knowing he would soon feel the joy of release, he opened his eyes to check out the wrestling.

He decided to grin and bear the lost time, the empty space, the utter futility, knowing he would reap the rewards. It was 10.26. He would sit here until midday, breathing deeply, drinking constantly, exercising his shoulders, neck, hips and lower back regularly and with increasing vigour. Then he would be set up for the day.

He looked carefully around the room, searching for something new, for recent additions, for signs of reluctant submission to change, but found none. The sofa bore the unmistakable signs of a long, remorseless life, its arms tired and balding. The sideboard marked the march of time with cold, detached obedience, its edges blackened by busy hands and wilful neglect. The rug showed the same familiar stains, defiled by guilty parties, soiled by shared memories, discoloured by the relentless onward charge of passing seasons. He could feel the weight of time, the burden of belonging, the fear of familiarity, though with a hard-fought, stubborn optimism he opened the curtains to let in the light.

He was feeling much better, so he made some toast and a cup of tea. The kitchen was safer territory. It was a place for planning, preparation, for practical things. He still had £11.02 on his key tray (formerly an ashtray, until smoking in the house was banned). He decided to take a fiver and all the loose change from his wage packet, to allocate £3 max for the bookies (he would probably do a Lucky 15, 20p per bet, depending on the going), to put a £5 note in his new savings envelope (still empty and thrown casually into the top drawer of his dresser) and to save the rest for Sunday, subs and weekday expenses. Executing the plan carefully and with well-practised precision, he smiled in satisfaction at the positive outcome, pleasantly surprised at the bonus afforded by forgotten bits and pieces.

The lure of the day was irresistible, so he decided to get ready earlier, before the water in the tank got too cold. He took a shallow bath to wash his hair, hands, face and feet, using a freshly boiled kettle to top up the tepid water. He dried off, brushed his teeth, scrubbed his nails and cig fingers in the sink, combed his hair and took the clean clothes from his allotted section of the bottom shelf in the airing cupboard. He selected his outfit for the day before carefully distributing the other items of fresh laundry to their correct positions in the wardrobe, drawers and dressing table. He dressed, grabbed his jacket from the wooden hanger fastened to the hook on the wall (for display purposes) and was ready for the world. He checked his airways, pressed an index fingertip against each temple, rested his chin on each shoulder, and was satisfied.

It was still morning when he stepped out into the street, though the sense of release and hopeful expectation outweighed any threat of potential embarrassment. He was restored and walked with an air of distinction, leaving each passing gate trailing in his wake, dismissing every front door, pouring scorn on the kerbstones and fractured pavement. The day was alive with possibility, buzzing with the silent song of the unexpected, bright with the invisible light of opportunity. He checked his pockets. He felt the comforting brush of coins against his right thigh, the velvet touch of age-worn banknotes on protective hands, the reassuring embrace of the door key nestled in his inside pocket, resting on his heart. He was shielded from harm, sheltered from pain, safe in the knowledge of wage slips, track listings, phone numbers, starting prices and beer towels.

Feeling optimistic, and despite it not being his favourite, he decided to nip into the local bookies as it would be easier to pick up on Monday if needs be. It was almost empty, though the air was bristling with a studious, business-like charge. A handful of punters analysed the weights and distances, calibrating significance. Good going everywhere. Faithful to a longstanding but unfounded superstition, he picked a horse in each of four consecutive races at the same meeting, listing the names and times on the slip in his best handwriting, as a recent hard-learnt lesson had taught him. He carefully checked the serial number on the slip, took it to the counter, asked to take the prices, watched hawk-eyed as the bookie wrote down the prices, and paid with his three dirtiest and most dog-eared pound notes (he liked to save the best for last). He collected and carefully checked the details on the bottom copy, watching discreetly to check that the bookie filed the master copy in the corresponding pigeon hole. All above board!

It was just gone midday, and the live commentary was yet to start, so he made a swift exit. To avoid the indignity of punctuality, he decided to walk to town.

He walked slowly and deliberately, desperate not to break a sweat as it would be a long day. The streets were familiar, friendly, unremarkable, and he was struck by an uncharacteristic sense of attachment. The contemptuous edges of the copings and ridge tiles were dulled by the bright expectation of the day. He walked across roads he'd once ridden down, past houses he'd once been in, along lanes he'd hitherto avoided, amidst memories, amongst absent friends, with ghosts, over the footbridge. The familiar fears were assuaged, though, as he could feel the firm foundations, sense the strength of the cornerstones, and knew he would keep walking. Plus, he had over forty-four hours left to play with.

He arrived at The Feathers at 12.52, having dismissed the need for confirmation phone box stop-offs on the way down. Noticing Daz and Danny safely ensconced at the usual table, he felt a fleeting flush of vindication and bought a drink. The other Shaun and the other Shaun's older brother, Chris, turned up shortly after, and the stage was set.

The early afternoon was a triumph. The beer went down slowly, and the cigs were shared sparingly, but the mood was warm, intimate, conspiratorial. The bar fizzed with life, and the staff had their work cut out. The sun shone through the open curtains, casting a silver lining onto the lingering wisps of shimmering cig smoke, glazing the tops of tables, suffusing each lonely particle of airborne dust with a mysterious, vital energy. The room buzzed with a carefree, animated charge, its imperceptible power coursing between the legs of the bar stools, unfurling over the benching in the bay windows, hanging in the air above the bandit. This was what they worked for, what they waited for, what they deserved. Shaun felt victorious, liberated, accepted, connected, and strained not to smile on his way to the gents. Two hours passed in minutes.

It was approaching closing time, and at the bell, it was agreed that the afternoon would continue at Chris's house, following a well-deserved food break. Chris was hugely advantaged in having his own place but was constantly disadvantaged by having little real say in things. Shaun stepped out into the warm afternoon, cowering under the unforgiving glare of the burning sun in the open sky. Hands in pockets, head bowed, shielding his face from the unrelenting daylight, he led the way to The Station Diner – curiously located at a site lacking any visible signs of any station of any kind, past or present.

The place was packed with Saturday shoppers, and every table was taken, but years of shared experience kept them safe in the knowledge that multiple spaces would be vacated soon. As predicted, before long they were settled snugly at facing tables, a four and a two, with Daz's trainers occupying the empty seat. The dining room rang with the distant echoes of a disappearing world: a tartan shopping trolley, polythene headscarves, raincoats, snuff, an overenthusiastic frother, a fading photo, distressed Formica. Shaun was often ill at ease with sudden glimpses of the past, sometimes strangely attracted, sometimes fearful of the long shadows and dark corners, always wary of the dangers. He was living in the day, though, so he straightened the chair and pulled his chest up to the table. He was sure of his place, facing the future, happy to let go – plus the chips were good.

After washing down the final remains of their late lunch with the last of the stone-cold tea, the group stumbled clumsily back out onto the sun-baked pavement. Being the only one of the five legally entitled to, Chris was nominated to call in at the shop to buy some cans. For some reason, many under-eighteens regularly encountered dogged resistance to being served in shops, though strangely faced fewer difficulties in pubs, perhaps due to the benefit of the doubt given their sheer audacity.

Labouring under the uneven distribution of the additional load, they trudged wearily to Chris's rented back-to-back on Grosvenor Terrace, though the lightness of the mood eased the burden slightly for the negotiated but nevertheless reluctant bag carriers. Crashing in feigned exhaustion onto the sofa and occasional chairs, they each let out an exaggerated, affected groan, prompting a shared outburst of honest, unadulterated laughter, pure as the edible snow on milk bottle tops. Smiling in mutual recognition of the gravity of the moment, of the value in their common understanding, of the weight of responsibility in safeguarding the accumulated wealth of every trivial, inconsequential action, they each opened a can. Danny sipped the overflow from the rim as he took control of the record player.

In the depths of the lull, in the shallows of shared silence, as they sunk into the chairs, the day reached its peak. Shaun slumped into an unnatural, disfiguring position, using his stomach as a table for the can and ashtray. He could feel the tension in his neck gently dissipate as it sought release through the collarbones and shoulders, the strain in his lower back easing into the thinning upholstery, the pain in his joints dissolving into the blood. His eyelids were heavy, though the leaden mass that tormented the bridge of his nose was gradually lifted, its stubborn particles crumbling, evaporating, floating away. The music filled the room with its irresistible, all-merciful power, its unifying force felt stroking the fading fabric, seen snaking under polished pine, heard reverberating on machine-made marble. The five were as one, bound by unwritten laws, fused by invisible forces, unanimous in their agreement with things that were never said.

Shaun began to feel the strain, losing focus at times and increasingly struck by sudden losses of coordination. He rubbed his free hand against his face to stimulate the blood, rousing the rational, responsible side of his dual personality, taking deep breaths to keep this side lucid, straining his eyes to keep the other side at bay. An hour passed in a second. Eventually, the beer ran out, and it was agreed they would seek solace in the teapot and the videprinter.

"Are we gonna stay together tonight?" Danny asked.

"Not if Shaun does his usual trick!" Daz answered, meaning the other Shaun.

"We should agree to meet at The Duke for the last hour if we get split up. Then we can share taxis," Shaun suggested.

The others agreed, though the solemnity of their shared consent was punctured by a couple of knowing snorts and a subsequent ripple of subdued laughter, perhaps in recognition of the probability that a plan to reconvene after having split up was less likely to work than a plan to stay together throughout.

"I'm gonna go home to change my trainers," Daz declared.

"Yeah, me too," the other Shaun agreed.

"Might as well join you, or I'm stuck here with these two!" Danny added.

"The Feathers at seven?" Daz asked, not expecting an answer but anticipating a general aversion to dissent.

"C'mon, Sleeping Ugly!" Danny commanded, knowing that Shaun wouldn't want to be left behind to suffer Chris's supposedly funny videos, supposedly classic albums or supposedly fascinating collection of war memorabilia.

Pleasantly surprised by this unexpected opportunity to take a break, Shaun sighed in grateful exhaustion as he swilled his last slurp of tea. Giving due deference to the classifieds, the gang of four rose in respectful silence, facing the screen with common courtesy, standing to attention to await the slow conclusion of Scottish League Division Two.

The bell at St Mary's struck the quarter-hour as Shaun slammed the door. Upon exchanging pleasantries (or unpleasantries, in Danny's case), and thankful that this would take him in a different direction, he decided to call in at the bookies to check the results.

He walked down deserted streets, stumbling reluctantly through the outskirts of town, heading for the centre. The sun had gone, replaced by a broken blanket of summer stratocumulus, the disparate clusters conspiring to block out the light, the slowly merging mass casting a shadow of cold detachment onto the indifferent tarmac of empty roads. The daytime shoppers had headed for home, the night-time revellers were ready and waiting, the playtime kids had gone inside for their teas. It was the witching hour. The furniture warehouse stood lost and alone, its half-empty yard nostalgic for better days. The knitwear workshop slumbered in quiet contentment, counting sheep until Monday morning. The end terraces stood proud and statuesque, twitching in fear of betraying any signs of life within. Turning onto Viaduct Street, he felt the ghostly touch of abandonment on his neck and across his shoulders, and was frozen in time. He was walking past pictures, alone in a vacant set, a figure in a cardboard model. Approaching the bridge, he was released by the welcome attentions of a stray dog.

By the time he arrived at the bookies, the last race had weighed in, the board was complete, the racing pages had been pulled down, and the clerk had finally been left in peace to count the cash. To his amazement, he discovered he had picked two winners, a 3/1 and a 7/2, both second favourites. Before anyone could say 'Jack Robinson', he had calculated that four and a half times 80p equalled £3.60, plus £1.70 equalled £5.30, take away just over 50p equalled just less than £4.80 (he always took off 10%, rather than 9%, as not only was it easier to work out, but it also left a little bonus). He double-checked his bottom copy twice to further verify details he was already 100% certain of before returning it safely to his inside pocket, fastening the button in smug satisfaction, keeping it secure until Monday when he would collect on his way home.

He looked in pity on the last few sad punters as they shuffled regretfully amongst their own losing slips. His work was done, so he made a sharp exit, grateful to pull clear from those who had fallen behind, those who had tailed off, those who had refused.

As it was too far to go home and come back, as he only had seventy minutes, as he already had his shoes

218

on, as the sun had returned, as his clothes were still relatively stain-free, as he needed to come round a bit, he decided to kill time in the Jubilee Gardens. He bought a potted meat sandwich and a can of limeade from the bakery just before closing and took up position on one of the wooden benches lining the herbaceous borders.

He thought he would spend his time wisely, thinking. He would start the first part of his qualification this year, knuckle down, set himself up nicely for the main part. Then he would be able to get a better job, get away from pick lists and packing. He needed to sort out his clothes: get a few new bits, sell a few old bits, do a few repairs. He needed to organise his music: borrow and tape a few, lend a few in return (to restore his dwindling reserves of goodwill), make a few radio compilations, tape-to-tape a few cassettes and sell the originals.

He needed to split his savings – one lot for up to and including Christmas, the other lot for next summer. He would go abroad again, this time ditching the family. He would get a train and then swap, as the coach would be allowed onto the ferry, which would thereby be included in the price of the ticket. He'd find somewhere to stay when he got there. He'd just walk. He'd buy beer from the supermarket and sit in the park, or walk by the river, or shelter in the shade of statues, watching the traffic negotiating the roundabouts. In the evening, he'd go up to the big church on the hill. He'd find a good vantage point on the steps and look out over the lights of the city, listening for the promise of the night, feeling the wind on his face, searching for signs of life, drinking beer from bottles.

The town hall clock struck the half-hour. Having decided to set off at the count of seven – not only to mark the precise moment at which thirty-eight hours remained, but also to lengthen the odds of being the first to arrive – he was resigned to killing time in the marketplace. He checked the prices in the window at the travel agents, not in hope but suspecting he ought to know these kinds of things, in case they came up. He searched for properties in the window at the estate agents, looking for houses he recognised, memorising the addresses. He examined his reflection in the window at the tobacconists, ceremonially wiping down the front and sleeves of his jacket, carefully adjusting his cuffs and collar, proudly modifying his stance and posture, which had begun to show strain under the weight of the afternoon. He tested his eyes on the wrappers and labels, flexing the muscles to exorcise the spectre of sudden sleepiness, taking a deep breath to draw it down into the lungs, exhaling in triumph as it diffused into the blood.

He felt fantastic! As the clock struck the hour, though, he decided to call in at the shop for another can of limeade and some precautionary painkillers.

Distrustful of the spirit of good humour, he knew he might be grateful for both in an hour or so. He retraced his steps through the same streets, though the stifling fear of the unknown had dissipated like the fading memory of vapour trails, leaving the cold contempt of familiarity trailing in its wake. The sun was starting its slow descent: fading colours, dulling edges, soothing hot surfaces, dimming the lights of the day. He stroked a passing window ledge, its soft stone surrendering under the relentless onslaught of the decades, its features numbed with old age. He felt the grains of sand on his fingertips, as hard as iron filings, as coarse as the morning in seafront bedsheets. He began to have doubts. To his sheer delight, though, the lampposts suddenly came on, both timely and premature, lighting the way.

He arrived at The Feathers at 19.19. As it was always quieter at the back bar, he nipped into the tap room to buy a drink before charting a course past the Ladies and into the lounge. Scanning the faces of the assembled cast with increasing annoyance, he slowly realised he was the first to arrive. To add insult to injury, their usual places were taken, so he took up residence at the table next to the bandit, which was often neglected due to the regular, unwarranted interruptions it warranted.

The room was already four-fifths full, though the early evening atmosphere was more formal, better behaved, less defiant. Eager girlfriends sat sipping their G&Ts, devouring weekly updates on scandalous workmates, their eyes and earrings glistening under the enchanting spell of shared youth. The jacket and tie brigade sat at their usual spots, taking huge quaffs of white-topped, mahogany beer, bristling in unison at what it said in the papers. Couples sat in silence, shifting uneasily under the unforgiving glare of restless sobriety, fidgeting in nervous anticipation of guaranteed release, trying to think of something to say. The air was clear, crisp and as yet untainted, though thick with a common expectation, and buzzing with quiet excitement as the fog of the night began to form in the dark corners and against the smoke-stained Anaglypta.

Danny, Daz and the other Shaun arrived at the same time. As Daz had clearly recommended meeting there at seven, thereby suggesting independent travel arrangements, Shaun wondered how, why, where and when the other three had met up. He wondered if they'd made arrangements to reconvene at a halfway point; or if one had called for a second who together had called for the third; or if they had just bumped into each other outside. He wondered what they had talked about when he left them two hours ago, and what they had talked about on the way there just now. He wondered where Chris was, too. Desperate to avoid appearing too eager, though, he had no intention of asking.

They were soon back in the swing of things. The dying day streamed in through raised sash windows and open doorways, flooding the carpet in the bewitching low light of late August. The congregation paid homage to the life-giving power of the setting sun, raising a glass in veneration, swearing devotion, lighting a cig in thanksgiving. A sense of elation was cast around the room, nourishing true believers and sowing the seeds of doubt amongst habitual doubters, as the spirits of the night leapt from table to table, putting words into mouths, animating faces, blowing bubbles, spiking drinks. It was a moment to cherish, filled with joy and remorse. This was the final act of the magic show of summer, before the schools went back, before the clocks changed, before the dark nights set in, before the dead leaves clogged up the gutter, before the busiest months at work, before Mischief Night, before the night after Mischief Night. Shaun raised an empty glass to someone he thought he vaguely knew and who he thought he had seen nodding in half-hearted acknowledgement from the other side of the room. Realising his mistake, he quickly took the drinks orders before cutting through to the back room, where he could check out the darts from the back of the queue.

Shuffling from one tiptoe to the other, constantly checking his watch (for visual effect), peering over both shoulders of the person in front, and beginning to wonder whether it was all worth it, Shaun was suddenly distracted by the sound of a fingernail tapping on glass. Danny was beckoning from outside, thereby confirming that it wasn't all worth it. By the time he had forced his way past the usual crowd of disappointed latecomers that hung around the doorway, the other three had left Shaun trailing by some distance.

He was glad to be alone for a while. It had been a long day, which was far from over, and he was beginning to fade, to dissolve, to disappear. Day was giving way to night. A fog of light fell upon the empty streets and deserted driveways, its unconvincing top canopy straining to brush the upper eaves and lower roof tiles, the comforting glow of the living room windows and the detached, impersonal glare of the lonely streetlights casting bottomless shadows into the brooding sky. He fought to keep the other three at a respectful distance, but nevertheless safely in view, breaking into fitful, lumbering sprints whenever they disappeared around corners, slowing to top walking speed whenever they re-emerged, beating a hasty retreat from the ghosts that haunted the drainpipes and cobblestones.

Marching relieved and triumphant into the welcome brilliance of the floodlit car park at the back of The Ship, Shaun noticed the other three waiting at the fire door.

"Thanks for waiting for me!" Shaun complained, sarcastically.

"You're welcome!" Daz replied, sarcastically.

"It's your round!" Danny added, sarcastically.

Shaun entered first and took up position at the back of the queue. The place was heaving and loud as hell. He waited impatiently as an angry mob jostled and jockeyed for position at the bar, before eventually ordering by sign language. Passing the drinks over the resistant heads of reluctant bystanders, he watched carefully as the other Shaun led the way to the shelter of the post at the bottom of the bannister at the foot of the steps to the mezzanine. Silenced by the impenetrable music, they each took regular, anxious, unappreciated sips of their drinks. Shaun could tell that the other three felt uncomfortable and smiled in well-disguised empathy as they shouted nervously at the sides of each other's faces, forcing themselves to make contrived, unnecessary, pointless, meaningless small talk.

He had mixed emotions. He felt awkward, out-of-place, self-conscious, uneasy, but was determined to remain aloof, detached, above-it-all. He scoffed at the blinding lights, which merely served to illuminate the ubiquity of the dull and colourless. He turned his nose up at the expensive aftershave, balking at the unmistakable scent of obedience, acquiescence, compliance, servility. He mocked the ear-splitting music, which only highlighted the dumb, deafening silence between them. He took long, scornful, contemptuous swigs, focussing every last nerve and sinew of his wrist, elbow and shoulder, on keeping a steady hand, desperate for a sharp exit.

His wish was soon granted. Danny downed the dregs of his drink before indicating a relocation to The Duke with a single flick of the thumb. Shaun and the other two followed suit, and they were soon back in the cool, comforting company of the kerbstones. Night had fallen from the sky, leaving an empty, terrifying space in its vacated place. Shaun sensed the suggestion of a stumble, so he stopped to start again, setting his sights on the lights. He led the way across the road, desperate for the guaranteed safety of the other side, the warm consolation of familiarity, the welcome shelter of the dazzling downlighters, which beckoned like school nativity stars.

They were soon settled snugly in one of their many favourite spots. Shaun was glad of the temporary relief from drinks responsibilities, as he was starting to falter. Seeing a friendly face through the window, though, he went outside to chat, joining a group of three. They were talking about cars, which wasn't his strong point. He thought of a way in, though realising it was a little late in the month, he decided to reword his approach.

"Did you see a W reg on the first day?" he asked.

An animated conversation about makes, models, colours, costs, suppliers, countries of origin, sighting locations and observed directions of travel ensued, quickly followed by an in-depth analysis of the corresponding TV adverts. Daz passed him a drink, then went back inside. Then they talked about cigs, someone listing the prices of those that were cheap at the station shop, someone else identifying the costs for various packs of two hundred when passing through Duty Free on the return from Spain. Shaun shared his French tobacco pouch multi-pack story, and someone else recommended good locations for the purchase of separates. Then they talked about beer, someone confirming the best shops in which to get served (which the others already knew), someone else comparing the relative merits and costs of sweet and dry cider. Shaun recounted every detail (yet again!) of his French supermarket case of twenty-four cans anecdote, and someone else listed the top five lagers. Danny passed him a drink, then went back inside. Someone left the group, and someone else joined. Shaun took a seat on the wall, thereby indicating his intention to observe and listen and perhaps to contribute only sparingly. Then they talked about music, someone listing the songs on the commonly favoured Side Two of a mutually admired album (Shaun interjecting with undisguised delight to provide the name of the easily forgettable fourth track of six, universally derided as a filler). Someone else name-dropped the influences, someone else suggested a more coherent and reasoned order of play. The other Shaun passed him a drink.

"It's every man for himself now!" the other Shaun confirmed, then went back inside.

Shaun became distracted. He looked out into the road, following the passing taxis until they eased into the turning onto Dalton Street, their brake lights casting a crimson coating over the double yellows. The flags in the showroom courtyard fluttered in the strengthening breeze, their tired, neglected edges shredded by westerlies. He could see a white streetlight at the far side of a distant stretch of unfamiliar fencing. Why was that one white? Why was it different? He could see the Tech, and beyond to the library, and beyond to whatchamacallit. Coming round a bit, he realised he'd been abandoned. Leering through the window to check on Danny, Daz and the other Shaun, who had all disappeared, he felt the gentle nudge of a partial, fragmentary sense of self-awareness.

Better sort himself out. *Could count the cash. No, should have plenty left, plus it's bad manners to count in public. Shoes have got some funny marks. Don't know what happened there! Should go back inside, have a wander around, look for them three. No, they must have split up, otherwise they'd still be sat together at the window seats. Shouldn't just butt in if they've started something up with another crowd. Wouldn't know which one to go to anyway. Plus, it's best to sit down. Play it safe! Could go and sit down inside, in the corner, behind the bandit, where it's always quiet. Getting a bit cold outside. Yeah, inside, behind the bandit.*

The lights behind the bar shone like a hundred miniature suns, shattering the bottles in the optics into a million dazzling shards, scattering fake diamonds into the folds of the cut glass decanters, casting a golden sunset onto the burnished copper drip trays. The lamps in the lounge were low and subdued, beckoning strangers into the warm, reassuring shelter of their halo shadows. The dark corners of the ceiling tiles, lonely and neglected, missed out as usual. The benches in the bay window began their slow, almost imperceptible orbit of the pumps, as they did twice, sometimes three times every week.

Someone stood on Shaun's grave. Resurfacing with a start from the deep pool of sleep, in which he had started to sink, he realised some time had passed. He looked for clues, though everything appeared as it was: unchanged, timeless. He glanced casually at the groups at the neighbouring tables, taking long, deep, restorative breaths in the hope that his actions had gone unnoticed. He was in the clear, seemingly. He was beginning to feel a bit better and harboured ambitions of a second wind. With immaculate timing, Danny and Daz returned to save the bacon.

"Where you been?" Danny asked.

"Taking it easy. I've had a hard day!" Shaun replied.

"We're moving on. You coming?" Daz asked.

"Yeah, sure," Shaun replied, not bothering to enquire about the other Shaun.

Danny and Daz led the way through the double doors and down the stone steps, leaving Shaun to bring up the rear. The back door of the taxi was left open, awaiting his arrival. He climbed in carefully, straining to act normally, trying to move purposefully, hoping to be able to speak clearly, if needed. As the car pulled away, he closed his eyes in nervous anticipation of motion sickness before blinking in stunned surprise at its apparent complete absence.

He leant against the door, staring absentmindedly through the window. Lampposts hurried by unnoticed, casting flashes of thin, sickly, pale amber pallor across his indifferent face. Shopfront windows reflected the illuminated signs of neighbouring stores, the lurid, vulgar, garish splashes of primary colours seeming brash and misplaced amongst the abandoned, empty paving stones. Cars passed by on the other side of the road, going the other way.

The taxi pulled up at the front of the queue, much to Shaun's annoyance. One of the bouncers stood in the light of the doorway, shrugging in disapproval. The driver was oblivious, focussing instead on collecting a pound from two of his three passengers. He insisted on notes, which were eventually offered by Shaun and Danny. The meter showed £1.30, so Shaun waited for the change. Quickly calculating the lowest amount he could offer as a tip whilst also leaving a final total that was evenly divisible by three, he reluctantly suggested the driver gave him back 50p. Shaun kept the change, and Daz gave 50p to Danny. All sorted.

Climbing begrudgingly from the warm, reassuring security of the faux leather seats, they emerged like naughty children into the stark, unforgiving light of the lobby and cloakroom area, cast out onto the pavement like belligerent drunks. Shaun gave a gesture of apology to the scowling bouncer (flicking his thumb to suggest that it was the driver's fault, nodding in deference towards the back of the queue, raising his palms to the sky to suggest that taxi drivers were a law unto themselves, that they didn't care, that there was no point in saying anything, that they just did what they wanted anyway), and received a pair of raised eyebrows by way of partial exoneration. They lumbered in embarrassment down the one-sided gauntlet of impatiently waiting clubbers, feeling like second years caught trying to push in at the front of the dinner queue (as soon as they got their feet under the table, that lot thought they ran the bloody place).

Thankfully, the queue had shrunk at an uncharacteristically steady pace, and they were soon parting with an additional 50p. Climbing the stairs to the first floor, Shaun felt the first flush of disdain, the cold touch of contempt, the cruel stroke of self-inflicted bad luck. He had been here a million times and felt a hundred years old. He knew the best spot against the back wall, where the benching was still soft, and the light was just right. He had a favourite place at the bar, where the combined distance from the entrance and dancefloor improved the chances by 50%. He always used the same cubicle in the gents, where the seat still held firm and the lock on the door still worked. He had memorised the pattern of the assorted quadrilaterals on the carpet: blue and yellow, overlapping, red and orange, interlocking, blue and yellow, offset, red and orange, chequered. The music saved the day, though. He listened intently to the first bar of every song, making wishes. He let the full force of the chorus soar in his chest, wilfully submitting to every mocking, galvanising taunt in each line of the lyrics.

He stood at his favourite place at the bar and bought a drink before taking a seat in one of the dark corners, the best spot against the back wall (where the benching was still soft and the light was just right) having been taken. Danny and Daz appeared out of thin air and took up position on the adjoining benching. Shaun was relieved that his night's work was done. There was no pressure to impress in here, no need to keep an eye on the drinks, no reason to talk, no further responsibilities, no more worries. He slumped down in his seat, his head barely above table-level, settling in for the long haul. Observing from his lowly vantage point, he watched as the colours played chase across Danny's face, inducing a stunned hypnosis. Daz sat dazed and confused, mesmerised by the rainbow of emotions created by the refraction of music through cig smoke.

Shaun sat in the same position for two hours and fifty minutes, getting up only twice – once to buy another drink, a second time to use his favoured cubicle in the gents, (where the seat still held firm and the lock on the door still worked). It turned out to be a great night. Having endured a barren ninety minutes, the music really picked up. Danny and Daz, of course, abandoned him before the first beer had settled, though luckily three other people had come to speak to him during the course of the early hours: the first to seek advice about an impending release, the second to make enquiries about a mutual friend, the third to discuss the relative merits of home-brewed cider and American Strong Lager.

The last hour was the best. He spent most of it alone, keeping the beat with an invisible bass drum pedal, tapping his fingernails on the wooden shelf behind the headrest, thinking about the trip to the city (which he had neglected to mention to the others) and picturing himself in distant, imaginary places (sheltering in the shadow of a bridge, the cars overhead lining the route out of the city, danger lurking in the darkness, a constellation of city stars reflected in the deep, deceitful water).

The lights came on, and everybody left. Outside, he made a woeful attempt to locate Danny and Daz before heading for home. He decided to walk again. It was Saturday, so he was in no mood to rush. An angry crowd of belligerent drunks had gathered under the unforgiving neon glare of the sign outside the taxi rank, rudely defending their places in the utterly dishevelled queue. Shaun couldn't for the life in him understand where everyone was going that was so special, or why everyone was so desperate to get to bed, or what everyone had to get up early in the morning for. It all seemed so pointless. He decided that he might as well put up with it now, as he'd be glad he did it in the morning. Plus, he had the whole day tomorrow!

He walked the first two miles through the tunnel of his own thoughts, oblivious to the purr of the late-night taxis, the glow of the landing lights, the eyes of prying insomniacs. He was in a confused state, hopeful and regretful, frustrated and fulfilled, animated and exhausted. He kept his eyes on the long-deserted pavement, relishing the rare reappearance of self-awareness, wallowing in the muddy luxury of consciousness – concentrating. Realising where he was, he decided to focus on his feet, watching in fascination as they swung to and fro unprompted. He counted to eight repeatedly, hoping to get home quicker without moving any faster. Bored of that, he looked all around, but there was nothing to see apart from the all-too-familiar emptiness of everything being exactly as it always had been.

It was the dead of night, the darkness of an impenetrable sky deepening under the weight of the vast emptiness of space. The air seemed clearer, though, and things seemed less fuzzy. The lines in the brickwork looked clean and distinct, the columns of lampposts proud and unbowed, the cracks in the pavement crisp, fresh and unadulterated. The invisible fog of the previous day had cleared, revealing the cloudless, unblemished promise of a new dawn. He zipped his jacket up to the top to shield his chest from the wind that cursed the estate road, raising his collar over his neck to complete the look, as was customary.

Eventually, and at the vastly reduced limits of imagined endurance, he arrived at his final destination, throwing his key into the ashtray in limp submission. The table was strewn with souvenirs from the family trip to the coast, which he realised would indicate a complete absence of leftovers in the fridge. Crestfallen, he made a crisp sandwich and poured himself a glass of milk from one of the bottles of red-top.

Night was giving way to day, the pale light of morning indicating its imminent arrival on a tyre-worn patch of tarmac at the turning into The Birches. Everything was silent and still. The things on the table seemed discarded and dismissed, as if abandoned in the race to the bathroom, like a makeshift memorial to a day to remember, like a still life. The taps stood to attention, dry as a bone, the fridge sat in the corner, cold as stone, the caddy sheltered the tea bags, all alone. Outside, the lampposts cast a vacant sheen on the driveways, lawns and panelled fencing, wasting the last of their light on the empty spaces above the gravel and between the houses. Everything was silent and still.

Shaun shuffled up the stairs and tiptoed into the bathroom. He brushed his teeth before checking his eyes, lips, gums and jawline in the mirror. Staggering to the bedroom, he threw his clothes in an untidy pile on the chair, draining every last drop of energy into a tortuous attempt to hang his jacket up neatly, which was partially successful. He climbed into bed, exhaling in uncharacteristic, exaggerated satisfaction. To his disappointment, and although he was utterly exhausted, he didn't feel sleepy, which he knew from bitter experience was something altogether different. To make things worse, birds started to sing.

He lay motionless, listening to the ringing in his

ears. Looking at the piles of assorted junk, stuff, clutter, scrap, trash, dross and other arbitrary, indiscriminate, seemingly priceless valuables that were randomly scattered around the top of his dresser, he noticed the comb of a harmonica staring back from under a pack of permanent markers. It was the harmonica he bought at the caravan site. He decided that, if he didn't get to go abroad next summer, he might grin and bear it with the family for a week after all. He could go to the secret beach with Si, getting down via the local dog walkers' route and climbing back up on the knotted rope, if it was still there. He could walk along the tops, using his dad's binoculars to follow the slow progress of the oil tankers and to look for seagulls' eggs in the nests that clung to the cliff face. At night, they could all go to the club, and he could play air-hockey and Derby Day with Si before sneaking a couple of drinks on the outdoor decking, like he did when he was fifteen.

8

The Silent Wind

Si woke with a start, shaken by the uninvited appearance of the morning sun. In a state of needless panic, he shielded his eyes to check that his new shoulder bag was still hung in prime position on the back of the bedroom door. Reassured, he slumped back down into a lying-in-bed-because-you-can't-be-bothered-to-get-up position. His dad had paid the full amount for the bag, shunning Si's offer to go fifty-fifty and allowing him instead to use his £2 in savings as spend for the day. Plus, all the kids had been given an unexpected £1.50 by the coach driver's assistant on the way over. Plus, he'd taken 16p in emergency loose change. Plus, he'd found at least twenty 2s that had either been abandoned unnoticed or had dropped unsupervised into the Tuppenny Falls winnings trays during the course of the afternoon. So, he'd had a great day! He wasn't allowed to touch the bag until the evening, though, when it was time to get ready for school. His dad said that if he started messing about with it, then he'd probably break the strap or smudge the lettering or turn it into a pile of dust just by looking at it.

Resisting the temptation to stay in bed and eager to please, he climbed cautiously down the stairs, careful not to fall. His dad was pottering about outside, his mum was pottering about in the kitchen, and Shaun was still in bed (obviously), so the living room was deserted. The unmistakable veneer of Sunday morning covered every surface. The tabletop shone like the lake behind the water tower, the ripples of grain showing flashes of gold, the drop leaves saturated in the proud light of affordable luxury. The hearth wore the stains of the week, the tiles showing tell-tale signs of misuse, the coasters awaiting realignment. The TV screen displayed a thin layer of dust, the particles hanging loose with gravity-defying resolve, clinging to the memory of long-gone static. Everything was frozen in time because everything that had happened had happened in the past, and everything that was going to happen was going to happen in the future. He went into the kitchen to make some jam butties and a pot of tea.

"Hi, Simon. You tired today?" his mum asked.

"Yeah, a bit," he replied.

"Ah well, bath and then early to bed tonight," his mum added.

"Yuppidoo times two!" he moaned.

Finishing his butties in seconds flat, he lumbered back into the room and took up position on the sofa, the back of his neck resting on one arm, the soles of his feet cushioned against the other, a mug of tea nestled carefully on his sternum. He pushed against the frayed upholstery at either end, squeezing the growing discomfort and accumulated tension from the soft spots between the vertebrae of his spine. It was Sunday, and he couldn't be bothered to get up to switch on the telly, as it would only be repeats of things that he didn't want to watch the first time around. He lay in bored silence, staring at the neglected ornaments on the mantlepiece, seeing them for the first time, though they had been there for centuries. A figurine in pastel shades stared blankly at unoccupied space, her Alpine costume fading unnoticed, her futile smile straining from the relentless ingratitude, dust gathering amongst the bread in her basket. Realising that today was in danger of darkening in the shadow of a glorious yesterday, he decided to get dressed and face the music. Strengthening in resolve, he diluted his tea with a drop of cold from the kitchen tap.

Five minutes later, he was out in the garden, having shot unnoticed through the kitchen to avoid being roped into the preparations for Sunday lunch. He was soon beginning to regret his rashness, though, as he was tasked with digging for potatoes. Slowly, and with due care and attention, he broke the sun-baked surface with his dad's time-worn fork, inserting the tines in the recommended position and at the customary angle of entry. Pulling the handle cautiously towards the ground, he snorted in relief as a respectable crop burst reluctantly to the surface. Throwing the main part of the harvest into Mum's old washing-up bowl (especially requisitioned for the purpose), he dug over the freshly broken ground with the trowel to tease out any escapees. Having been instructed to dig up a full row, he repeated the process five times, double-checking the newly created furrow with the spade upon completion before hoeing and raking the surface to leave a clean finish.

Having convinced his dad that the work had been done carefully and precisely as instructed, using the correct crop-maximisation measures and following the recognised collection and storage procedures, and that all the relevant tidying up jobs been completed to satisfaction, he was allowed to relax on the lawn. The unmistakable light of Sunday morning settled in slowly, lingering contentment on the petals of unknown flowers, softening the focus of the emerging day. Si felt the unforgiving sting of regret. He knew he would soon suffer the unmistakable light of a school day morning, when the early sun shines cold and emotionless on the kitchen sink and chequered lino. He knew he would soon endure the unmistakable light of late afternoon, when the lengthening shadows give false promise of respite on the tortuous walk home. He knew he would soon seek shelter in the unmistakable light of a curfewed evening, when the sweet smell of freedom is soured by the bitter taste of routine, restrictions and the inevitable shouts from impatient doorsteps. He knew, too, that none of this was anything to do with the light, or the weather, or the sun.

Heading back inside in limp resignation, he half-filled the big pan with water, added ten shakes of salt, and began grudgingly to peel some of the potatoes with a knife (starting, as always, with the medium-sized ones). He stared longingly out of the kitchen window. The sky was a timeless, deep blue, fading to a pale grey-tinged, brilliant white-washed, pure gold-flecked near-emptiness as it fell unnoticed to the horizon beyond the school playing fields. Birds danced on the tops of the trees beyond The Alders, oblivious to the world of pasts and futures. The silent wind crashed like summer breakers onto the teetering branches of the top canopy, clutches of wave-tossed leaves drowning in a shallow sea of deep green before resurfacing for air. Everything was as it should be, as it always would be, as he knew it soon again could be, though he struggled still to take it all in, to make it stick, to acknowledge the implications.

He decided to head out into the estate to try to shake off whatever it was that he couldn't decide was bothering him. He dropped the potatoes into the salty water, dumped the peelings into the bin, and left without a word.

Jase, Jay and Little Jay were standing in the middle of the street, oblivious to the danger. Si approached, at which point they headed off in the direction of the quarry, beckoning for Si to follow. As they marched a short distance ahead, kicking stones along the compacted gravel of the cut-through, Si analysed their body language for signs. Jase led the way with the calm confidence that comes with a September birthday, his head, neck and shoulders positioned to face the day head-on. Jay followed a little behind, a little to the right-hand side, but with the assured, defiant strut of someone not being led and most definitely not following. Little Jay danced along behind, happy to trail in their wake. Si's mood changed instantly, and he resolved to take on the challenges of the day with renewed conviction.

As it was getting close to dinnertime, they decided to do nothing, and selected a well-worn patch of compacted long grass for the purpose. Laying down (for effect), with fingers interlocked behind their heads (for effect), and with one leg crossed over the other (for effect), they completed the unfinished business of the previous day.

"You get anything yesterday, Si?" Jase asked.

"Yeah. My dad got me a new school bag and a new maths set and a new pencil case and some new pens and some new pencils and I got a pack of five C90s and some badges," Si replied.

"You spend up?" Jay asked.

"Yeah!" Si lied.

"I spent ages in The Funhouse. I was ninety up at one point, but I put it all back in. Then we walked along the front, all the way to the park. Mum gave us some of the bread that she'd brought for the chips, to feed the ducks, but me and Matty were throwing full slices in and we got told off by that guy who comes round with the collection for the driver – him with the shoes! Then we went on the beach. We just had dinner there and went in the water a bit, but it was freezing so we joined in with some others who were playing near the pier and then we just sat down for a bit and then we went back to The Funhouse and then we went up to town in the lift, and that's when we saw you," Jay explained.

Si and Jase each gave a detailed description of the previous day's events, with a few bits added, and a few bits missed out, and a few bits repeated for emphasis. Happy to draw a line under it, they made a collective agreement not to mention it again and to focus instead on the coming afternoon. They decided to make the most of their last full day of freedom, to meet up as soon as possible after dinner to maximise the available time, to look to the future, not to dwell on the past, and to call for the others before reconvening – all without saying a word.

After a dinner of chicken, boiled potatoes, carrots, cabbage and peas, Si headed straight back out into the street, temporarily forgoing dessert. He stood at the three-way junction of Alder Avenue, Birch Crescent and the top end of the estate road, where he knew his visibility would be maximised. Out of nowhere, Jase appeared with four others in tow, having presumably assumed responsibility for knocking on doors. Si spotted that, of the usual suspects, Jules was the single absentee, no doubt for one of the usual reasons. With suppressed excitement and admirably concealed fascination, Si asked Matty where he had found the car tyre that he was carrying, merely to receive a mischievous shrug of the shoulders by way of response.

Si, Jase and Jay retook their previous positions on the flattened grass at the top of the quarry, Matty and Pete leading Little Jay down the hill to the railings at the top of the railway embankment. Si went first, closing one eye in an affected attempt at taking careful aim before rolling the tyre down the hill towards the trio of human targets. Everyone howled as the tyre crashed against the railings, missing Pete by six feet. Si knew there was no real danger, that the boasts of suffering a near miss were grossly exaggerated, and that it wouldn't hurt that much anyway. The laughter, though, was pure gold, forged in the joy of conspiracy, the ecstasy of unity, the euphoria of pretence.

Si took two more turns before handing over to Jay. The grass was warm and inviting, its bowed seed heads nodding in consent. Si rested on his left forearm, searching the closest clumps for good chewers. He laughed as the charade grew ever more ridiculous, as the act was slowly exposed, as Little Jay stood in motionless salute before the approaching missile, only for it to miss again. He looked across at Jase, who looked back. They shared a smile. It was a smile of acknowledgement, in recognition of the harmony within the group, and in appreciation of the unspoken closeness between the two of them.

The game having run its natural course, most of the group were happy to skip the customary swapping of roles. Only Little Jay insisted on taking a turn at rolling, the five older boys creating an unmissable target before writhing in feigned agony as the tyre vaulted up against the top rail, much to Little Jay's delight. Pretending to notice a gap in the railings which everybody actually knew about and had used several dozens of times, Jay led the way down the railway embankment.

Naturally, and with little planning or coordination, they stepped seamlessly into the long-established routine of the railway: tightrope walking against the clock, marching in tune to the sleepers, playing chicken, listening to the rails for the mesmeric, other-worldly promise of the distant approach of non-existent trains. They each placed a coin on the rail at a spot easily recognisable from its position in relation to the nearby signals, vowing to return the following week to conduct a search (it cost Si 6p, Jay and his brother being empty pocketed). Matty was convinced he could hear a train coming, sending some of the others into a confused panic (not so much as to whether a train was actually coming or not, but rather as to whether he was kidding or not, and therefore what the appropriate response might be). Si knew, though, that there were only a couple of trains each week and never on a Sunday. If there was the faint suggestion of a distant, slowly approaching train, Si knew it was just the sound of the rest of the world, existing somewhere else.

Escaping the imagined danger of the rails via the unofficial dirt track that climbed steeply up the left-hand side of the moor road bridge, Si took the lead, casually directing the group towards the relative safety of the park. He knew it wasn't a day for accidents, or for getting lost, or for seeing something that someone would have to do something about, or for getting into trouble, or for being followed by a dog. Most of all, it wasn't a day for being somewhere where they shouldn't be and someone saying or doing something to them which they wouldn't have said or done to them if they hadn't been somewhere where they shouldn't have been.

They took a shortcut through the deserted playground with the paint-stripped climbing frame. After careful consideration, Si concluded that it was less than a week since they had last been there, though it seemed like a million years ago! They walked slowly uphill, past the so-called castle wall, The Wheatsheaf, the quarry steps, the pony field (with its laughably insecure barbed wire fence), the cobbled alley that ran past the mill cottages and, finally, The George, eventually emerging, relieved and exhausted, onto the welcome familiarity of the park road. They called in at the newsagents to buy some pop and sweets, Si bungling his unconvincing attempt to cry poverty for a second time by openly counting six coins to the value of 26p. Officially the newsagents was shut, but the door was wide open, and the newsagent was pottering about behind the counter, so he reluctantly relented.

Entering the park through the gap in the fence next to the much more easily accessible and permanently open side gate, they sauntered over the imaginary by-line of the imaginary football pitch before crashing in an uncoordinated but universally acceptable arrangement into the long grass of the imaginary centre circle. Si looked up to check the clouds, and the sky, and the sun.

He caught a glimpse of an easier road ahead. He saw the light of something reliable, something permanent, something relentless, something under which everything else and everyone else and every other time and every other place diminished, lessened, shrunk. He saw it in the flashes of fire that flecked the colossal shoulders of the spiralling, swelling, slowly condensing water. Gradually plucking up the courage, over three or four minutes or so, he decided to speak, unprompted.

"We'll still have a couple of months of light nights, and we'll have to be in before dark anyway for most of them, so we won't miss that much yet. Then we'll start collecting wood for the fire, so we don't really need the light for that. In fact, it's better in the dark cos it's easier for raiding and for hiding everything. Then there's the birthdays, and then it's nearly Christmas, and then it starts getting lighter again," Si said, hoping to adequately convey his eternal faith in the Earth's endless orbiting of the Sun, its perpetually skewed rotation, and the resultant ceaseless cycle of the seasons. No-one responded.

Deciding to spend the remainder of the afternoon in the park, everyone went home to get stuff and to ask if they could stay out a bit longer, bearing in mind they wouldn't be allowed out after tea (they were all allowed out on every other evening before a school day, even in the middle of winter, but not on the evening before the first day of each term). Soon they were all reassembled, this time over by the barbed wire fence, which was the customary place for making piles of coats, hanging surplus jumpers, and abandoning things for later use. Jules made an appearance, having been collared by Jase during one of his regular inspections of the front gardens, thus guaranteeing full attendance.

First, they played tennis, accessing the courts through the gap in the fence that the parkies were clearly aware of but had decided to overlook, given the slim chances of attracting paying customers. They played doubles, with an umpire at the net and a line judge at opposite sides of each end. After much deliberation, Si was chosen to play continually, as it was agreed that his middling ability would probably produce a greater degree of equity, impartiality and technical balance. He was therefore excused from officiating. Shunning the traditional scoring system – which they saw as silly, contrived and unnecessary – they played first to eleven, players from alternating pairings taking turns to serve five times, before swapping roles and ends at the conclusion of each game. Si realised that swapping ends was silly, contrived and unnecessary as, other than him, it was different players every game, and they shouldn't have to swap just for his benefit, but he didn't say anything. Si was pleased with his game, despite the perennial problem of his weak backhand nudging the ball disappointingly into the net. Luckily, he was the weaker player in each of the pairings that he played in, and on each occasion, his partner, acknowledging the admission of inferiority, allowed Si to play on the right-hand side.

Next, they played football. Si was tired and would have preferred to be goalie, but Jase had already secured the position by using one of the many universally recognised verbal claims to precedence. As there were seven players, they played three-a-side, single goalie, first to three, one player from each side swapping at the end of every game, thereby ensuring the original teams were re-established at the end of every three games. Si hung around towards the back of the unmarked but somehow scrupulously observed playing area, shunning glory for a less physical, distributive role. After thirty minutes, though, the pain began to tear into his chest, the weight hung heavy in his legs, and all the oxygen in the air had been used up, leaving only nitrogen. He picked up the ball, thus accelerating the inevitable process by which the game descended from a deadly serious, highly competitive physical encounter into a light-hearted, theatrical, semi-comedic free-for-all.

Next, they played Commando. This involved one player closing his eyes and counting to thirty whilst the others hid behind trees, in the bushes, and under anything it was possible to crawl under within the available time. The football was chosen as the 'base' to which the hiders had to try to return without being tagged by the seeker, which was always easiest when the seeker was searching for someone else. Anyone who successfully returned to base remained a hider in the next round, with those tagged by the seeker joining him in the search for the hiders in the next round. The ultimate aim was to become the solitary remaining hider, which was sometimes possible, though it was a role with zero chance of success. The game had a series of unwritten rules. For instance, if there were only two or three seekers, it wasn't acceptable for one of the seekers to stand and wait at the base, preventing any of the hiders from successfully returning. However, if there were more than three seekers, it was understood that one seeker would remain at base, at which point the aim of the game was to be the last remaining hider to be found. It was a bit like hide and seek, though nothing at all like hide and seek, as that was for little kids.

Little Jay was nominated as the first seeker, and Si hurried to a spot where he was familiar with the wall-side arrangement of a knot of neighbouring bushes, confident in the knowledge that he was the only living human with an intimate understanding of the intricate interplay between the branches of the undergrowth. He peered out through a gap in the curtain of leaves, waiting for Little Jay to appear in his line of vision. He felt furtive, subversive, conspiratorial, as if observing the target of an ongoing clandestine operation from somewhere removed, remote, afar. Everything looked unreal, imagined, out-of-focus, like the muted, grainy images on the portable when the dial needed a delicate, cautious, barely perceptible minor adjustment. The target disappeared out of sight, and he was alone with the flowers. He rubbed the lower leaves of a hydrangea between his palms to disguise the scent, though he knew this was utterly pointless. To his amazement, Little Jay, standing triumphant behind him, tapped a victorious finger on the top of his head. Resurfacing onto the safety of the tarmac, they laughed in unison at the sight of the others passing the football in a five-pointed star sequence.

Having each retired unannounced from the unforgiving relentlessness of the afternoon, they were soon resting exhausted against the cool luxury of the chain link fencing, the shadow of the barbed wire piercing a line of holes across the bell-bottoms of their jeans. They busied themselves with doing nothing. Si scratched cryptic symbols into one of the innumerable, rain-starved bald patches by the invisible corner flag with the perfectly suited tip of a well-chosen piece of border gravel. Jay cleaned scuff marks off the ball with a judiciously licked index finger and the out-turned right pocket of his jeans (the rest of his jeans being too dirty to leave a clean finish). Jase hunted for lolly sticks in a desperate and ultimately fruitless search for one with a joke worth sharing. Jules threw a stone to make a target, then threw another stone at his target stone, then threw more stones, the target stone changing with unseemly regularity, depending on where his most recent stone landed. The other three sat cross-legged, each picking grass from the shadow of their right leg and throwing the cuttings into the space between their ankles, unconsciously mirroring each other with uncanny synchronicity. It was the perfect ending to a perfect day.

Si looked up to take in the view. Everything seemed to be coming to an end. The trees that sheltered the park road bid a final farewell to the benches lining the perimeter path, the leaves of the lower branches heaving like storm-tossed waves, breaking in flashes of sunlit green by way of late summer salutation. The distant long grass of the Wasteland swung to and fro in reluctant resignation, heads bowed in muted acceptance. The clouds stole away towards the east, sloping off surreptitiously with a priceless booty of gold, diamonds and silver linings, leaving behind only grey. Everything looked like the last day of something. Si felt the piercing pain of sadness. He couldn't wait for tomorrow evening, when it would all be over, and everything would be brand new again.

Jay and his little brother were the first to call it a day, closely followed by Matty, Pete and Jules, all three of whom were rarely willing to take the initiative but always keen to follow suit. Si and Jase decided to cut their losses, making an unspoken agreement to waste time at every given opportunity as they began the slow trudge towards home.

Jase stopped off at a lamppost to show Si the various sets of double initials carved into the time-worn top stone of the adjoining garden wall, though they were both aware of the ownership of, history of, and every exaggerated legend associated with each pair of letters. Si stopped to pick up a beer bottle top, identifying the relevant brewery before quickly naming five pubs in the area which were tied to the same brewery, the three other main regional breweries, a couple of local pubs tied to each of those, and finally, the best-selling beers and lagers made by each of the four several times aforementioned breweries. Jase stopped again, this time to list the occupants of the pair of semis at the other side of the street and to relate various interesting facts about them and to describe several unusual features of them.

"Mitch in the year above lives at number six. His little sister is mates with Matty's little sister. My Auntie Jill used to live there before she moved to the coast. She left all the beds and stuff when she went, and Mitch has the bedroom that I used to sleep in when I stayed over.

The loft has floorboards and sockets and stuff, as my auntie used to do her photos up there. Hardy in fifth year lives at eight. He doesn't have any brothers or sisters or anything, so he's got the big bedroom at the back. His mum is friends with Pete's mum, and me and Pete went in there once when she took some curtains round. There's a tropical fish tank next to the table and chairs at the back of the kitchen, and there's a piano in the hallway," Jase explained, in greater detail than he'd ever explained anything ever before.

They limped the last leg of the inevitable return at record slow speed, taking baby steps and stopping several more times so as to better explain various pointless ideas to each other with exaggerated, theatrical, time-consuming hand gestures. Jase eventually bid his final farewells, though, having decided to take a debatable shortcut down the alley directly opposite the alley that led to the school playing fields.

Si looked across to the empty sky above the deserted corridors of the new annex building. The space in-between had lost all sense of foreboding to the unstoppable approach of the everyday, the ordinary, the mundane. A piercing speck of brilliant white light hung low and lonely above the horizon, beyond the line of trees at the crest of the quarry. At first, it seemed to slowly flicker, as if approaching, or as if gradually disappearing from view, or as if fluttering in fear of continuous explosions of volatile, superheated gas. Then it seemed to sit stone still, as all that surrounded it quivered and shivered, trembling in awe of its terrifying, unforgiving power. Having carefully considered all the options, though, he realised in dismay that it was merely the late light of the setting sun burning bright in the broken reflector of the floodlight at the back of the staff car park.

Befitting her legendary status as the estate's leading culinary clairvoyant, Si's mum laid his plate on the table the moment he stepped in through the kitchen door. In an oft-used gesture of silent sympathy and unspoken understanding, she'd also poured him a big glass of yellow lemonade. After an uncharacteristically unhurried tea of tinned salmon, two boiled eggs, tinned potatoes and a stick of celery, Si retired to his bedroom.

The sun had begun its slow descent. The shadow of the chimneypot crawled with chilling, perceptible stealth across the rain-starved back lawn, inching menacingly ever closer to the greenhouse. The threat of autumn hung in the air, sending shivers down Si's spine. The open window inhaled a cold, calculated forewarning of winter, the hairs on Si's arms standing on end. The last of the sun flooded the landing, pouring in through the front bedroom windows. The frame of Shaun's half-open door cast a golden pyramid onto the woodchip, its tip illuminating a time-worn patch of bathroom lino – the opposite of a shadow. The summer was in retreat, withdrawing along Alder Grove, cutting through the alley, and dropping like a stone to the foot of the quarry before pulling back in defeat across the wild, desolate moor, following the lines of lonely pylons towards distant, unknown territory.

Mum skipped up the stairs and into the bathroom, singing her relentless, uncompromising song of good cheer as she ran the bath.

"Nearly seven o'clock, Simon," she proclaimed as she rearranged the towels in the airing cupboard, meaning that he might as well accept his fate, that there was no escaping it, that it wouldn't be that bad, and that he might as well get it over and done with. Leaving Si to face the inevitable, she made a tactical retreat.

Although his mum had closed the living room door on her way back to finishing up in the kitchen, Si could still hear shifting and shuffling in the hallway. From the hushed tones of the slow, deliberate movements, from the begrudging groan of the bills and bankbooks drawer, from the deep, baritone moan of the long-suffering floorboards, Si could tell it was his dad.

"Dad! Can I sort my bag out now?" he asked optimistically.

"OK! But go easy on the zip. It's more haste, less speed where zips are concerned," his dad replied.

Si jumped up and rushed over to his bedroom

door, where the new bag hung in suspense on the dressing gown hook. He carefully checked the contents, eventually noticing an unexpected paper bag. Pulling out a brand new sixty-watt light bulb, he almost shrieked in unbridled, unanticipated joy.

"Sixty-watt!" he boasted out loud, in barely disguised delight.

Printed in Great Britain
by Amazon